Harlequin ◆ Romances

OTHER
Harlequin Romances
by BETTY NEELS

Many of these titles are available at your local bookseller,
or through the Harlequin Reader Service.

For a free catalogue listing all available Harlequin Romances,
send your name and address to:

HARLEQUIN READER SERVICE,
M.P.O. Box 707, Niagara Falls, N.Y. 14302
Canadian address: Stratford, Ontario, Canada N5A 6W4

A Gem of a Girl

by

BETTY NEELS

Harlequin Books

TORONTO • LONDON • NEW YORK • AMSTERDAM • SYDNEY • WINNIPEG

Original hardcover edition published in 1976
by Mills & Boon Limited

ISBN 0-373-02063-5

Harlequin edition published April 1977

Printed in U.S.A.

CHAPTER ONE

Gemma was at the top of the house making beds when she heard the ominous shattering of glass. The boys were in the garden, kicking a football around, and she wondered which window it was this time. She mitred a corner neatly; news, especially bad news, travelled fast, someone would be along to tell her quickly enough.

It was George, her youngest, ten-year-old brother, who climbed the three flights of stairs to break it to her that it was Doctor Gibbons' kitchen window. 'And I kicked it,' he added with a mixture of pride at the length of the shot and apprehension as to what she would say.

'A splendid kick, no doubt,' declared his eldest sister robustly, and shook a pillow very much in the manner of a small terrier shaking a rat. 'But you'll all have to help pay for the damage, and you, my dear, will go round to Doctor Gibbons when he gets back from his rounds, and apologise. I'll telephone Mr Bates in a minute and see if he'll come round and measure up the glass right away—perhaps he might even get a new pane in before Doctor Gibbons gets back. But you'll still have to apologise.'

'For a girl,' said George, 'you're not half bad.' With which praise he stomped downstairs again.

She heard him in the garden a few moments later, arguing with his brothers as to the sum of money required for the new window pane.

Gemma finished the bed and went, in her turn, downstairs. She was a smallish girl and a little plump, but nicely so. Her hair, hanging down her back in a brown tide loosely tied with a ribbon, was the same soft brown as her eyes and although she was on the plain side, when she smiled or became animated, the plainness was lost in its charm. She was almost twenty-five years old and looked a good deal younger.

She went straight to the telephone and besought Mr Bates to come as soon as he could, and then retired to the old-fashioned wash-house adjoining the kitchen, and started on the week's wash; a fearsome pile, but she was used to that; with three boys in the family and two sisters younger than herself, there was naturally a vast amount.

She eyed it with a jaundiced expression; it was a pity that Mandy and Phil had gone to friends for the weekend—of course she could leave it until the next day when they would be back, but the Easter holidays ended within a day or so and it seemed mean to blight their last freedom with a lot of hard work. Besides, it was a lovely day, with just the right kind of wind. She battled with the elderly washing machine and then left it to thunder and rumble while she went to the kitchen to make coffee. It would be a relief when Cousin Maud got back from her visit to her brother in New Zealand—five weeks, reflected Gemma, of holding down a full-time job,

6

running the old-fashioned house and keeping an eye on her brothers and sisters was just about her limit; thank heaven there was only another week to go—less than a week now, she remembered happily as she went to stop the machine. She hauled out the wash and shoved it into the rinser, set it going and then filled the tub up again. The two motors, working in unison, made the most fearful noise, but she was used to that, merely reiterating to herself the promise that one day she and Cousin Maud would get another washing machine, as she went back to the kitchen to drink her coffee.

She was back in the wash-house, hauling out the first batch in blissful silence, when a faint sound behind her caused her to say: 'George? or is it William or James? take some money from the housekeeping jar and get some sausages from Mr Potter—and don't waste time arguing about going if you want your dinner today.'

She was tugging at a damp sheet as she spoke, and when a strange voice, deep and leisurely, said: 'I'm afraid I'm not the person you think—my name's Ross,' she dropped it to shoot a startled look over her shoulder.

She had never seen the man standing in the doorway; a tall, broad-shouldered individual, with pale hair which was probably silver as well, she wasn't near enough to see, but she could see his eyes, blue and heavy-lidded below thick, pale brows. He had a high-bridged nose and a firm mouth and he was smiling. He was a very good-looking man and she stared for a moment. He bore her look with

7

equanimity, laid a football which he had been carrying on a pile of sacks by the door and remarked: 'Your brothers', I believe,' and waited for her to speak.

Gemma disentangled the sheet and heaved it into the basket at her feet. 'You're from Doctor Gibbons,' she stated, and frowned a little, 'but you can't be the foreign professor who's staying with him; the boys said he was short and fat and couldn't speak English ...'

Her visitor shrugged. 'Boys,' he remarked, 'I've been one myself.' He smiled again and Gemma wiped a wet hand down the front of her jersey and skipped across the floor between them.

'I'm Gemma Prentice,' she told him, and held out a hand, to have it engulfed in his.

'Ross Dieperink van Berhuys.'

'So you are the professor. Do you mind if I just call you that—your name's rather a mouthful, isn't it? For a foreigner, I mean,' she added politely. 'And thank you for bringing the football. I do hope it didn't disturb you—the window being broken, I mean. They all go back to school tomorrow.' She gave him an unaffected smile. 'Would you like some coffee? If you wouldn't mind waiting while I load this machine again ...?'

His thank you was grave and his offer to hang out the clothes ready for the line was unexpected; she accepted it without arguing and he went into the large untidy garden with the basket while she switched on once more and went back into the kitchen to fetch another mug.

8

The coffee was freshly ground and carefully made; she and Cousin Maud cooked and baked between them and they both turned out what her older relation called good wholesome food; the coffee she poured now smelled delicious and tasted as good as it smelled. Her unexpected guest, sitting comfortably in an old Windsor chair, remarked upon the fact before asking gently: 'And you, Miss Prentice?'

'Me what?' asked Gemma, all niceties of grammar lost; if the boys had disappeared—and heaven knew they always did when there was a chore to be done—she would have to leave the washing and fetch the sausages herself, which meant she wouldn't get her work done before dinner. She frowned, and the professor persisted placidly, 'The sausages bother you, perhaps?'

She gave him a surprised look. 'How did you know?' She refilled their mugs. 'Well, actually, yes ...' She explained briefly, adding obscurely: 'I expect you're a psychiatrist—they always know things.'

Her companion turned a chuckle into a cough. 'Er—I suppose they do, but you did mention sausages ... I'm an endocrinologist, myself.'

He got to his feet, his head coming dangerously near the low ceiling. 'I should be delighted to fetch these sausages for you while you finish your washing.'

He had gone before she could thank him, and was back again in a very short time, to put his parcel on the kitchen table and observe: 'There is someone repairing the window.'

'Oh, good—that'll be Mr Bates. I asked him to come round as soon as he could—it's so much nicer for Doctor Gibbons if he doesn't see the damage.'

The professor's lids drooped over amused eyes, but his voice, as he agreed with this praiseworthy sentiment, was as placid as ever.

'I daresay you find it difficult to understand,' she went on chattily, 'but it's impossible not to break a window now and then when there are three boys about the place.'

Her companion made himself comfortable on the edge of the kitchen table. 'I don't find it in the least difficult,' he protested. 'I'm the eldest of six, myself.'

Gemma flung the last of the washing into the basket. Somehow it was hard to imagine this not so very young man in his elegant casual clothes being the eldest of a large family—and they would surely all be grown-up.

Just as though she had spoken her thoughts out loud, her companion went on smoothly: 'I'm thirty-seven, my youngest sister is not quite eighteen.'

'Phil's as old as that ... the twins are thirteen and George is ten. Mandy's twenty.'

'And you are twenty-five,' he finished for her. 'Doctor Gibbons told me.'

'Oh, did he? Would you like some more coffee?'

'Thanks. I'll hang this lot up while you get it, shall I?'

'Well, I don't know about that,' said Gemma doubtfully. 'You're a professor and all that; I daresay you don't hang out the washing at home so I don't see why you should here.'

His blue eyes twinkled. 'No, I can't say I make a habit of it, but then I'm working for most of my day when I'm home.'

It was on the tip of her tongue to ask him about his home and if he was married, but moving very fast for such a sleepy-eyed person, he was already going down the garden path.

She didn't see him for the rest of that day and she left the house at half past seven the next morning, cycling through the quiet country lanes to get to the hospital a couple of miles away.

Mandy and Phil had got back from their weekend late the previous evening; Gemma had called them before she left the house and they would get the boys down for breakfast and off to school and then get themselves away; Phil to her coaching classes before school started—she was in her last term and working for her A levels—and Mandy to the library in Salisbury where she was training to become a librarian. Gemma, pedalling down the road at great speed, was aware that it was a glorious May morning —a morning to be free in which to do exactly what one wished; she cast the thought aside and bent her mind to the more mundane subject of what to cook for supper that evening, the chances of getting the ironing done, whether the twins could go another week before she need buy the new shoes they wore out with terrifying frequency, and behind all these thoughts even though she kept nudging it aside, the wish to see more of the professor. He had been kind and easy to talk to, and Gemma, the plain one of the family and always conscious of that fact, had been aware that he hadn't looked at her with the faintly amused surprise with which those who had already met the rest of the family—all of them possessing good looks—were wont to show.

She rounded the entrance to the hospital and slowed down to go up the neglected, grass-grown drive, casting, as she always did, an admiring glance at the building coming into view as she did so.

The hospital wasn't really a hospital at all; many years ago it had been a rather grand country house with a fine Tudor front, which had been added to by succeeding generations, so that there was a Queen Anne wing to the left, a charming Regency wing to the right, and round the back, out of sight, and a good thing too, was a mid-Victorian extension, red brick, elaborate and very inconvenient. But with the death of the heir during World War Two and crippling death duties, the house had been sold to the local council and had been used as a geriatric hospital ever since. It was, of course, most unsuitable; the rooms were either too lofty and huge and full of draughts, or so small and awkwardly shaped that the getting of elderly ladies in and out of them, not to mention the making of their beds, was a constant nightmare for the nurses.

Gemma propped her bike against a convenient wall and went in through an open side door, into a narrow, dark passage and up a back staircase. There were two Day Sisters looking after the fifty-six patients; herself with thirty old ladies in her care, and Sister Bell, who was housed with the remainder of them in the opposite wing.

Gemma went up the stairs two at a time, changed into uniform in five minutes flat, standing in a cupboard-like room on the landing, and then, very neat and tidy in her blue uniform and starched apron, an equally well-starched cap perched on her bun of brown hair, walked sedately across the landing into another cupboardlike apartment, which Authority allowed her to use as an office. Both the day and night nurses were there waiting for her to take the report, and she greeted them in her quiet voice, bidding them to sit down as she squeezed herself behind the table which served her as desk. The report hardly varied from day to day; Mrs Pegg and Miss Crisp fell out of their beds with monotonous regularity despite the nurses' efforts to keep them safely in—they had both done so again during the night; there weren't enough nurses for a start and old ladies could be very determined. Lovable too.

When Gemma had given up her post as Medical Ward Sister in a big London teaching hospital, she had done so with many private misgivings; it had been expediency, not choice, which had caused her to apply for the post at Millbury House. Cousin Maud, who had looked after all of them for some years by then, was beginning to show signs of wear and tear—and who wouldn't? Gemma had spent all her holidays and days off at home so that she might help her, but it hadn't been enough; once Mandy and Phil were off their hands, things would be easier, but until then, it had become a matter of urgency that someone should help. That was six months ago and although she missed the rush and bustle of the big hospital, Gemma had to admit that she didn't dislike her work; besides, it had made it possible for Cousin Maud to go to New Zealand for the long-dreamed-of holiday with her brother. Gemma, heartily sick of doing two jobs at once, couldn't wait for her to get back.

The night nurse safely on her way, Gemma and Sally Black, the day staff nurse, separated to start their day's work. The main ward was a long room with windows down its length, overlooking the gardens at the side of the house; at one time it must have been a drawing room, for its fireplace, now no longer in use, was ornate, gilded and of marble, and the ceiling was picked out with gilt too. Gemma trod from one bed to the next, having a word with each of her patients in turn, handing out a woefully sparse post, listening to the old ladies' small complaints, and occasionally, cheerful chatter. Almost all of them were being got up for the day; a ritual which they, for the most part, objected to most strongly, so that the two nursing aides who came in to help part-time were constantly hindered. Gemma finished her round, quite worn out with her efforts to persuade her patients that to get up and trundle along to the day room across the passage was quite the nicest way of spending their day, but she really had no time to feel tired. She took off her cuffs, rolled up her sleeves and sallied forth once more to tackle Mrs Pegg and Miss Crisp, who now that they might legitimately leave their beds were refusing, with a good deal of noise, to do so.

The day went quickly enough. Nothing dramatic happened; the old ladies were dressed, given their meals, their medicines, bathed, chatted to whenever there was time to spare, and then prepared for bed once more. It was visiting time after dinner, but only a handful of people came. After the eager rush of visitors who had invaded the ward Gemma had had in London, she felt sad, even after six months, that the very people who needed visitors seldom had them. True, some of the old ladies had no family at all, but there were plenty who had who could surely have come more often than they did. Millbury House was some miles from Salisbury, but there was a bus service of sorts, and anyway, most people had cars these days.

She made a point of walking round the wards while the visitors were there so that anyone who wanted to inquire about Granny or Auntie could do so, but they seldom did. When the last of them had gone she went to her office and started the Kardex so that Sally would only have the last few details to fill in later on, and it was while she was doing this that she was interrupted by the house doctor, a young man called Charlie Briggs. They discussed the patients one by one over a cup of tea, and because he didn't like her overmuch, he disagreed with everything she had to say; he almost always did. When she had first arrived at the hospital he had heralded her appearance with delight. 'Thank God,' he had said, 'someone under forty at last—now perhaps life will be fun!' He had eyed her at such length that she had coloured faintly and then

disliked him forever when he exclaimed: 'Oh, lord
—I do believe you're good as well as plain.'

They had to meet, of course, but only during the
course of their work. She had often thought wryly
that it was just her luck to work with a man who
didn't like her at all—a young man, not married, he
might have fallen for her, who knew? they might
have married ... She had laughed at herself for
having the absurd notion, but the laughter had
been wistful.

She was tired by the time she was ready to cycle
home just before six o'clock. Phil would be home, so
would the boys, but Mandy wouldn't leave the
library for another half an hour. She wheeled her
bike round to the shed at the back of the house,
called a hullo to the boys as she passed the sitting
room where they were doing their homework, and
went to the kitchen. Phil would be upstairs in her
room, deep in her school books, but she had left a
tray of tea ready on the kitchen table for Gemma.
She drank it slowly, sitting in the Windsor chair
with Giddy, the family cat purring on her lap,
before starting on the supper. The boys had peeled
the potatoes and seen to the vegetables and she had
made a steak and kidney pie the evening before;
she went and got it from the fridge now and put it
into the oven before going to the cupboard to see
what she could serve for a pudding. She had the off
duty to puzzle out, too, she remembered; she had
brought it home with her and could have a shot at
it while the supper cooked. She fished the book out
of her cardigan pocket and sat down at the table,

conscious that she didn't want to do it at all; she wanted to sit in a chair and do nothing—well, perhaps not quite nothing. It would be nice to have time to sit and think; she didn't admit to herself that what she wanted to think about was the professor next door.

She wasn't on duty until eleven o'clock the next morning; she saw everyone out of the house, raced through the housework and then pedalled through the bright sunshine to Millbury House, wishing with all her heart that she could stay out of doors. By the time she got off duty that evening it would be eight o'clock—dusk and chilly.

Her day was long and filled with little troubles. At the end of it she wheeled her bike through the open gate, stowed it for the night and went into the house through the kitchen door. There was a cold supper laid out for her on the kitchen table and coffee bubbling gently on the stove. She sniffed appreciatively and went on through the kitchen and down the passage to the sitting room where she found the boys bent so zealously over their books that she instantly suspected them of watching the T.V. until they had heard her come in. She grinned at them, said: 'Don't you dare until you've finished your lessons,' and went across to the drawing room. Phil would be upstairs, working, but Mandy would be there. She was, looking cool and incredibly pretty, and lounging opposite her was Professor Dieperink van Berhuys.

They both turned to look at her as she went in, and the thought crossed her mind that they were a perfectly matched couple, Mandy with her gay little face and curly hair and he with his placid good looks.

Mandy came dancing to her, bubbling over with high spirits, full of the news that the professor had happened to be outside the library when she had left it and had driven her home. She cast him a laughing glance as she spoke, and he, standing with his magnificent head almost touching the ceiling, smiled back at her, murmuring that it had been a pleasure and that now he really should go, for Doctor Gibbons would be wondering what had become of him.

Gemma said all the right things and watched him walk out of the room with Mandy. They didn't shut the door and she heard them talking in the hall and then go into the sitting room where there was an instant babble of talk and laughter. It made her feel suddenly lonely, which was absurd; how could she possibly be lonely with five brothers and sisters, besides the twenty-eight old ladies with whom she passed her days? Perhaps lonely wasn't the right word. She went back to the kitchen and sat down to eat her solitary supper, and presently she was joined by everyone else, crowding round the table to tell her about their particular day, eating a packet of biscuits between them while they did so. She wasn't all that much older, she thought, looking round at them all, but sometimes she felt just as though she was the mother of the family.

They went to bed one by one, leaving her and Mandy to wash the mugs and sweep up the crumbs and lay the breakfast for the morning, and all the while they were doing it, Mandy talked about the professor.

'He's almost forty,' she told Gemma, 'but he doesn't look it, does he? He's not married either, but his sister is—he's got two, the youngest one is as old as Phil, then there's a brother in his late twenties and another one who's in medical school, he's twenty-one.' She added thoughtfully: 'You'd think he'd be married, wouldn't you?'

Gemma wiped out the sink and put the cloth tidily away. 'Well,' she said slowly, 'with so many brothers and sisters, perhaps he can't afford to.'

'His mother and father are still alive.' Mandy perched on a corner of the table. 'He's got a simply super car ...'

'Perhaps he hired it.'

'No, it's his, it's got a Dutch number plate.' She smiled suddenly and brilliantly. 'He said I was a very pretty girl.'

Gemma pushed back her hair with a weary little gesture. 'And so you are, darling,' she agreed. 'We're a smashing lot of good-lookers except for me.'

'We all think you're lovely,' said her sister fervently, 'and depend on it, someone will come along and think the same.'

Gemma ate a biscuit. 'Then he'd better look sharp about it,' she observed cheerfully. 'All this waiting around doesn't do my nerves any good.'

They giggled together as they went up to bed, but presently, in her own room, Gemma sat down on the old stool in front of her dressing table and took a long look at her reflection. It didn't reassure her in the least.

She was persuading old Mrs Thomas to toddle across to the day room when she heard Doctor Gibbons arrive for his round the next day. He came regularly, for several of the patients had been his for years and he still came to see them. Gemma rotated her companion carefully and sat her down in a convenient chair and looked down the ward. Doctor Gibbons always had a chat with Mrs Thomas; she had no family left now and to her confused old mind he had taken the place of a long-dead son.

The doctor wasn't alone, his Dutch guest was with him, strolling along between the beds, saying good morning as he passed the elderlies while at the same time listening politely to Matron, sailing along a pace or two behind Doctor Gibbons doing the honours. Matron was a nice old thing, with mild blue eyes, a ready chuckle and a cosy figure. Gemma could see that the professor had her eating out of his hand.

The party reached her, exchanged greetings and settled down to the confused questions and answers which took the place of conversation with Mrs Thomas, leaving Gemma free to do something else. She went reluctantly, wishing that someone in the party—the professor, perhaps—would ask her to remain. But he didn't, only smiled his gentle smile and turned his attention to Matron, who was explaining about staff shortages, too many patients, the lack of amenities, the lack of visitors, the lack of transport ... Gemma, at the other end of the ward, assembling her medicine trolley, could hear the murmur of their voices.

Presently they came down the ward again and Matron went away and Doctor Gibbons started his ward round. They were the high spot of any day and this one was even better than usual, for Professor Dieperink van Berhuys came with them, asking intelligent questions, murmuring in agreement with his colleagues' more profound remarks, and now and again asking her, soft-voiced, her opinion of this or that. It gave her a real uplift when Charlie Briggs came importantly into the ward, to stop short at the sight of her in animated conversation with a man who put him, in every way, quite in the shade. He wasn't near enough to hear that they were discussing the use of water beds for the aged and infirm. She greeted him with dignity and was glad to see that, for once, he was less than his usual cocksure self. Perhaps that was due to the professor's impassive manner and Doctor Gibbons' brisk way of talking to him. Indeed, she began to feel sorry for him after a while, for he was showing off far too much and she strongly suspected that the professor was secretly amused; besides, there was the strong possibility that Doctor Gibbons would lose his patience with him and tear him off a strip. She was casting round in her mind how to deal with the situation when it was saved by the reappearance of Matron with an urgent message for Doctor Gibbons, and she was able to show the whole party to the door. She had closed it behind them and was making

21

for Mrs Thomas once more when the professor came back.

'Er—may I offer you a lift home this evening? I take it you're off at five o'clock?'

She stood looking up at him. He was being polite, of course, afraid that she had minded him giving Mandy a lift. He was really rather nice.

'How kind,' she said pleasantly, 'but I've got my bike here and I shall need it in the morning—thanks all the same.'

She smiled at him warmly and his answering smile was ready enough. 'Another time, perhaps?' His voice was casual, he made no effort to change her mind for her. With feminine illogicality she was annoyed. Her 'Goodbye, Professor,' as he opened the door was decidedly cool.

CHAPTER TWO

COUSIN Maud came home two days later, looking tanned and at least ten years younger—not that she was all that old; a woman in her forties was no age at all; Gemma had often heard Doctor Gibbons telling her cousin that, and had thought it to be a friendly platitude, but now, watching him greet her cousin, she wasn't so sure. She busied herself with welcoming sherry and speculated about that. Doctor Gibbons wasn't all that old himself—in his mid-fifties and as fit as a fiddle as far as she knew. True, he was a little thin on top and he wore glasses, but he must have been good-looking when he was younger—not, of course, as good-looking as his friend the professor. She nudged the errant thought on one side and concentrated on Cousin Maud and Doctor Gibbons. But even if they wanted to marry there were difficulties. He could hardly be expected to house the six of them as well as Maud. Somehow or other, mused Gemma as she passed the glasses around, they would have to manage on their own— after all, if it could be done for six weeks, it could be done for a lifetime. She shuddered strongly at the very idea and then consoled herself with the certainty that it wouldn't be a lifetime. Mandy would surely marry, so, in a few years, would Phil. James and John were clever boys, they would get their A levels and go on to university, and that left little George. Quite carried away, she began to weigh the chances of taking paying guests—with only George at home there would be three or four bedrooms empty, or perhaps Doctor Gibbons would offer George a home and she could sell the house, find a job and live at the hospital. The prospect was even worse than the first one. She frowned heavily and the professor said in her ear, very softly: 'What is it that worries you?'

She hadn't noticed him cross the room. He loomed beside her, smiling his gentle smile, his pale brows slightly lifted.

'Nothing,' she said hastily. His vague 'Ah', left her with the impression that he didn't believe her and she went on quickly before he persisted: 'Doesn't Cousin Maud look marvellous?'

He glanced across the room. 'Indeed, yes. And now presumably you will take a holiday yourself— you have been doing two jobs for the last six weeks, have you not?'

'Well—the others were marvellous, you know, and it wasn't easy for them; Mandy's away all day and so is Phil, and the boys did their bit.'

'Does Mandy not have holidays?'

She turned a surprised face towards him. 'Of course she does—four weeks each year, but no one could have expected her to stay home ...'

'Er—the thought did cross my mind—just a week or two, perhaps, so that she could have—er—shared the burden of housekeeping with you.'

'It wasn't a burden. I—I liked it.'

He had somehow edged between her and the rest of the room. 'That is a palpable untruth,' he observed mildly. 'Don't tell me that getting up with the birds in order to do the housework before spending the rest of your day looking after a great many demanding old ladies before coming home to cook the supper, help with the homework and generally play mother, was something you liked doing.'

He sounded so reasonable that she found herself saying: 'Well, I must admit that it was rather a full day, but I'll have a holiday soon.'

'You will go away?'

'Me? No.' He was asking a lot of questions. Gemma asked rather coldly: 'Would you like some more sherry?'

He shook his head and she need not have tried to interrupt him. 'You will stay here, fighting the washing machine, frying sausages and calling upon Mr Bates at intervals, I suppose?'

She smiled because put like that it sounded very dull. 'Cousin Maud will be here—she's marvellous ...'

They both turned to look at that lady, deep in conversation with Doctor Gibbons. Perhaps, thought Gemma, it might be a good idea not to pursue this conversation. 'When do you go home?' she asked chattily.

'Earlier than I had intended. Rienieta, my youngest sister, is ill and at the moment there's no diagnosis, although it sounds to me like brucellosis—her fever is high and she is rather more than my mother can cope with.'

'I'm sorry, it's a beastly thing to have—I had several cases of it when I had a medical ward.'

'So Doctor Gibbons was telling me. You must find the difference between an acute medical ward and your old ladies very great.'

'Yes, I do—but they need nursing too.' She added honestly, 'Though it isn't a branch of nursing I would choose. It's convenient, you see, so near home ...'

'You are on duty in the morning?'

She nodded. 'Yes, but wasn't I lucky to be able to get a free day so that I could be home to welcome Cousin Maud?'

Her companion let this pass. 'I'll take you in the morning,' he stated. 'I have something I wish to say to you.'

Her eyes flew to his face, but it was devoid of any clue. 'Oh—what about?' She paused, remembering that he had taken Mandy in and out of Salisbury several times during the last few days, and besides that, she had come across them deep in conversation at least twice. Perhaps he had fallen in love with her? He was a lot older, of course, but age didn't really matter; perhaps he just wanted to discover what she thought of it. She said matter-of-factly: 'I leave at ten to eight on the bike.'

'A quarter to the hour, then. That will give us time to talk.' He moved a little and Phil came over to join them, and presently Gemma slipped away to the kitchen to see how the supper was coming along.

It was pouring with rain the next morning when she left the house, so that she had wrapped herself in a rather elderly mac and tied a scarf over her head, which was a pity, for her hair, although it didn't curl like Mandy's or Phil's, was long and fine and a pretty brown. But now, with most of it tucked out of sight, her unremarkable features looked even more unassuming than usual, not that she was thinking about her appearance; she was still puzzling out a reason for the professor's wish to speak to her—a reason important enough to get him out of his bed and go to all the trouble of driving her to the hospital. Well, she would know soon enough now. His car, an Aston Martin convertible, was outside the gate and he was at the wheel.

She wished him good morning in a cheerful voice, wholeheartedly admired the car and got in beside him and sat quietly; the drive would take five minutes, and presumably he would start talking at once.

He did. 'I shall be going home in a week's time,' he told her without preamble. 'I should like you to return with me and look after my sister for a week or so—they have confirmed that she has brucellosis and she is in a good deal of pain and her fever is high. My mother assures me that she can manage for the time being, but Rienieta is sometimes very difficult—she refuses to have a nurse, too, but I thought that if you would come with me and we—er —took her unawares, as it were, it might solve that problem. She's a handful,' he added judiciously.

'Well!' declared Gemma, her eyes round with surprise while she hurriedly adjusted her ideas. 'I

27

didn't expect ... that is, I had no idea ...' She perceived that she would get no further like that. 'I can't just leave Mellbury House at a moment's notice, you know,' she pointed out at length.

'I had a word with Doctor Gibbons,' said her companion smoothly. 'He seems to think that something might be arranged for a few weeks—unpaid leave is what he called it.'

'Why me?'

'Because you are the eldest of a large family, I suppose, and know just how to deal with the young.'

She felt like Methuselah's wife and said with a touch of peevishness: 'I'm twenty-five, Professor.'

The amused glint in his eyes belied his placid expression. 'I beg your pardon, I wasn't thinking of you in terms of age, only experience.' He slowed down to turn the car into the hospital drive. 'Of course, if you dislike the idea, we'll say no more about it.'

She didn't dislike it at all, in fact she felt a rising excitement. She held it in check, though. 'It doesn't seem fair on Cousin Maud.'

'She hasn't the least objection. Doctor Gibbons happened to mention it to her yesterday.' He drew up outside the side door. 'Think it over,' he said with maddening placidity, 'and let me know. We're bound to see each other during the next day or so.'

His goodbye was so nonchalant that Gemma told herself crossly that nothing, absolutely nothing, would make her agree to his request even if it were possible to grant it, which seemed to her very unlikely. Moreover, she would keep out of his way, he really had a nerve ... she shook off her ill humour as she walked on to the ward; it would never do to upset the old ladies. All the same, she was a little distraite, so that old Mrs Craddock, who had been there for ever and knew everyone and everything, exclaimed in the ringing tones of the deaf: 'And what is wrong with our dear Sister today? If I didn't know her for a sensible girl, I would say she'd been crossed in love—her mind isn't on her work.'

It was a good thing that her companions were either deaf too or just not listening. Gemma laughed, told Mrs Craddock that she was a naughty old thing and went to see about dinners. Mrs Craddock liked her food; her mind was instantly diverted by the mention of it. Gemma gave her two helpings and the rest of the day passed without any more observations from the old lady.

It was towards the end of the afternoon that she remembered that she hadn't got her bike with her and the professor had said nothing about fetching her home; the nagging thought was luckily dispelled by the appearance of Doctor Gibbons, who arrived to see a patient very shortly before she was due to go off duty and offered her a lift. 'Ross told me he had brought you over here this morning, so I said that as I was coming this afternoon, I should bring you back—that'll leave him free to go into Salisbury and pick up Mandy.'

Gemma smiled with false brightness. The professor might appear to be a placid, good-natured man without a devious thought in his head, but she was beginning to think otherwise; he had had it all nicely planned. Well, if he thought he could coax her to ramble over half Europe he was mistaken. Her sensible little head told her that she was grossly exaggerating, but she cast sense out. Holland or Hungary or Timbuktoo, they were all one and the same, and all he was doing was to make a convenience of her. Her charming bosom swelled with indignation while she attended to Doctor Gibbons' simple wants with a severe professionalism which caused him to eye her with some astonishment.

Cousin Maud had tea waiting for her, which was nice. Everyone was out in the garden, picking the first gooseberries, and the professor was there too, although long before Gemma had finished her tea he had strolled away. To collect Mandy, Cousin Maud explained with a smile, so that Gemma, on the point of asking her advice about the professor's request, thought better of it. She wasn't really interested in going to Holland, she told herself; she wasn't interested, for that matter, in seeing him again. She could not in fact care less. She looked so cross that her companion wanted to know if she had a headache.

Gemma was upstairs when the professor returned with Mandy. He didn't stay long, though, and she didn't go downstairs until she had seen him get back into his car and shoot out of their gate and into Doctor Gibbons' drive. She could see him clearly from her bedroom window; indeed, she was hanging out of it, watching him saunter into the house next door, when he turned round suddenly and looked at her. She withdrew her head so smartly that she banged it on the low ceiling.

For the time being, she didn't want to see him. Let him come again and ask her if he was so keen for her to nurse his sister, and it was really rather absurd that she should leave her old ladies just to satisfy his whim. She tidied her already tidy hair and sighed deeply. Probably she would be at Mellbury House for ever and ever—well, not quite that, but certainly for years. She went slowly downstairs, the rest of the evening hers in which to do whatever she wished, and she was free until noon the next day, too. She wouldn't see her old ladies until then.

She saw them a good deal sooner than that, though. Several hours later she was wakened by the insistent ringing of the telephone. She had been the last to go to bed and had only been asleep for a short time, and it was only a little after midnight. The house was quiet as she trod silently across the landing and down the stairs, not waiting to put on dressing gown or slippers. Doctor Gibbons' voice sounded loud in her ear because of the stillness around her. 'Gemma? Good. There's a fire at Mellbury House—they've just telephoned. Matron's pretty frantic because the fire brigade's out at another fire and they'll have to come from further afield. Can you be ready in five minutes? Wait at your gate.'

He hung up before she could so much as draw breath.

She was at the gate, in slacks and a sweater pulled over her nightie and good stout shoes on her feet, with a minute to spare. The house behind her was quite still and the village street was dark with not a glimmer of light to be seen excepting in the doctor's house, and that went out as she looked. Seconds later she heard the soft purr of the Aston Martin as it was backing out of the drive and halted by her. The professor was at the wheel; he didn't speak at all but held the door open just long enough for her to get in before he shot away. It was left to Doctor Gibbons, sitting beside him, to tell her: 'The fire's in the main building, the first floor day room. It'll be a question of getting everyone out before it spreads to one or either wing.' He turned to look at her in the dark of the car. 'The fire people will be along, of course, but if all the patients have to be got out ...' He paused significantly and Gemma said at once: 'There's Night Sister, and a staff nurse on each ward and three nursing aides between them—and Matron, of course, as well as the kitchen staff, but I don't think they all sleep in.' She drew a sharp breath and said: 'Oh, lord, look at it!'

The night sky glowed ahead of them, faded a little and glowed again, and now, as the professor took the right-hand turn into the drive without decreasing his speed at all, they could hear the fire as well as see it and smell it. They could hear other sounds too, urgent voices and elderly cries.

The professor had barely stopped the car at a safe distance from the burning building than Gemma was out of it. 'It's my ward,' she cried, 'the wind's blowing that way. Oh, my dear old ladies!' She leapt forward and was brought up short by a large hand catching at the back of her sweater.

'Before you rush in and get yourself fried to a

crisp, tell me where the fire escape is?'

Gemma wriggled in a fury of impatience, but he merely gathered more sweater into his hand. As Doctor Gibbons joined them, she said urgently: 'At the back, where my wing joins the extension behind —there's a side door with a small staircase which leads to the landing outside my ward ...'

'The way we came the other day, from the centre door—that will be impossible now; the wind's blowing strongly from the centre towards your wing ... Is there a fire chute?'

'Yes—I know where it's kept.'

'Good.' He turned to Doctor Gibbons. 'Shall we try the side door, get into the ward and get the chute going from a window at this end? The fire escape is a good way away, I doubt if they can move the old ladies fast enough—if the dividing wall should go ...'

They were already running towards the house. In a moment they were inside, to find the staircase intact. 'Get between us,' said the professor shortly, and took the stairs two at a time, with Gemma hard on his heels and Doctor Gibbons keeping up gamely. The landing, when they reached it, was full of smoke, but although the fire could be heard crackling and roaring close by, the thick wall was still holding it back. The professor opened the ward door on to pandemonium; Gemma had a quick glimpse of the night staff nurse tearing down the ward propelling a wheelchair with old Mrs Draper wedged into it; it looked for all the world like a macabre parody of an Easter pram race. There wasn't much smoke; just a few lazy puffs curling round the door frame.

Gemma didn't wait to see more but turned and ran upstairs to the next floor where the escape chute was, stored in one of the poky, disused attics which in former days would have been used by some over-worked servant. The door was locked—she should have thought of that. She raced downstairs again, took the key from her office and tore back. The chute was heavy and cumbersome, but she managed to drag it out of the room and push and pull it along the passage to the head of the stairs where she gave it a shove strong enough to send it lumbering down to the landing below. But now she would need help; she ran to the ward door and opened it cautiously. The professor was quite near, lifting Mrs Thomas out of her bed and settling her in the wheel-chair a nursing aide was holding steady. He glanced up, said something to the nurse, who sped away to-wards the distant fire escape, and came to the door.

'I can't manage the chute,' said Gemma urgently. 'It's on the landing.'

He nodded, swept her on one side and went past her, shutting the door, leaving her in the ward. The beds, she noticed, had been pulled away from the inner wall and ranged close to the windows, and there were only six patients left. She sighed with relief as the professor came back with the chute and she went to give him a helping hand.

There was still only a little smoke in the ward, although the roar of the fire sounded frighteningly near. Gemma shut her mind to the sound and began the difficult task of getting Miss Bird, hopelessly crippled with arthritis, out of her bed, wrapped and tied into a blanket ready to go down the chute. The nursing aide had come back; she could hear the professor telling her to go down first so that she could catch the patients as they arrived at the bottom. The nurse gave him a scared look.

'I've never done it before,' she told him in a small scared voice.

The professor eyed her sturdy figure. 'Then have a go,' he said persuasively, and actually laughed. 'I've thrown a mattress down. Don't try to catch the ladies, just ease them out and get help, any help, if you can. And be quick, my dear, for the inner wall isn't going to hold out much longer.'

Gemma glanced over her shoulder. He was right; the smoke was thickening with every moment and there was a nasty crackling sound. She left Miss Bird to be picked up by the professor and hurried to the next bed—Mrs Trump, fragile, heaven knew, but very clear in the head, which helped a lot. She saw Nurse Drew plunge down the chute out of the corner of her eye, and a minute later, Miss Bird, protesting vigorously, followed her. She was ready with Mrs Trump by now and wheeled her bed nearer the chute and then wasted a few precious seconds dragging empty beds out of the way so that they had more room.

The professor already had a patient in his arms and she was tackling the third old lady when the wall at the other end of the ward caved in with a loud rumble, an enormous amount of dust and smoke and great flames of fire. Gemma, tying her patient into her blanket, found that her hands were shaking so much that she could hardly tie the knots. The professor was going twice as fast now, getting the next old lady into her blanket; she finished what she was doing and went to the last occupied bed—Mrs Craddock, apparently unworried by the appalling situation, blissfully unable to hear the noise around her. As Gemma rolled her into the blanket she shouted cheerfully: 'A nasty fire, Sister dear. I hope there'll be a nice cup of tea when you've put it out!'

Gemma gabbled reassurances as she worried away at the knots. The flames were licking down the wall that was left at a great rate now, and she could have done with a nice cup of tea herself. She was so frightened that her mind had become a blank. All that registered was that Mrs Craddock must be got down the chute at all costs.

The professor, elbowing her on one side without ceremony, tugged the webbing tight with an admirably steady hand and bent to take Mrs Craddock's not inconsiderable weight. 'Come along,' he said almost roughly, adding unnecessarily: 'Don't hang around.'

Mrs Craddock was stoutly built as well as heavy, and it took the professor a few precious moments to get her safely into the chute and speed her on her way. They were unable to hear the reassuring shout from below when she got there because the rest of the wall caved in with a thunder of sound. It did so slowly, like slow motion, thought Gemma, stupidly gawping it at, incapable of movement. The professor shouted something at her, but his voice, powerful though it might be, had no chance against the din around them. She felt herself swung off her feet and hurled into the chute. She hit the mattress at the bottom with a thump and a dozen hands dragged her, just in time, out of the way of the professor, hard on her heels.

The next few hours were a nightmare, although it wasn't until afterwards that Gemma thought about them, for there was too much to do; old ladies, scattered around in chairs, on mattresses, wrapped up warmly on garden seats—the fire brigade were there by now and a great many helpers who had seen the fire from the village and come helter-skelter on bikes and in cars; the butcher in his van, the milkman, Mr Bates and Mr Knott, the gentleman farmer who lived in the big house at the other end of the village. The only person Gemma didn't see was Charlie Briggs, who really should have been there and wasn't. She wondered about him briefly as she went round with Matron and Night Sister, carefully checking that each patient would be fit to be moved. Now and again she brushed against the professor, listened carefully when he bade her do something or other, and then lost sight of him again.

The beginnings of a May morning were showing in the sky by the time the last ambulance had been sped on its way, leaving a shambles of burnt-out wards, broken furniture and everything else in sight soaked with water. Those who had come to help began to go home again while Matron, looking quite

37

different in slacks and a jumper, thanked each of them in turn. Presently they had all gone, leaving Gemma and Doctor Gibbons, Matron, the night staff and the professor standing in what had once been the imposing entrance, while firemen sorted over the bits and pieces, making sure that all was safe before they too left.

It was the professor who suggested that he should drive everyone to their homes; Matron had been offered temporary shelter with the rector, whose house could be seen through the trees half a mile away, the rest of them lived round and about, not too far away, excepting for one nursing aide who came from Salisbury. He sorted them out, taking those who lived close by before driving Matron down the road to the Rectory. That left Gemma and Doctor Gibbons and the girl from Salisbury; he squeezed all of them into the car, left Gemma and the doctor at the latter's gate and drove on to the city. Gemma watched the car out of sight, yawned and started for her own garden gate.

'They've slept through it all,' said the doctor as he put out a restraining hand, 'they'd sleep through Doomsday.' He took her by the arm. 'Come in with me and make me a cup of tea. It's gone five o'clock; far too late—or too early—for bed now. Besides, there's no hurry, you haven't got a job to go to now.'

Gemma turned to look at him. 'Nor have I.' She waited while he opened the door and followed him inside; she knew the house as well as her own home; they had been friends for years now. She told him to go and sit down and went through to the kitchen to put the kettle on.

They had finished their tea and were sitting discussing the fire and its consequences when the professor got back. Gemma heard the car turn into the drive and went away to make more tea; probably he would be hungry too. She spooned tea into the largest pot she could find and sliced bread for toast. She didn't hear him when he came into the kitchen, but she turned round at his quiet 'hullo'.

'Tea and toast?' she invited, unaware how deplorable she looked; her slacks and sweater were filthy with smoke and stains, her face was dirty too and her hair, most of it loose from the plait by now, was sadly in need of attention.

The professor joined her at the stove, made the tea, turned the toast and then spread it lavishly with butter. He said to surprise her: 'How nice you look.'

Gemma stared at him over the tray she was loading, her mouth a little open. 'Me——?' She frowned. 'If that's a joke, I just don't feel equal to it.'

He took the tray from her and put it down on the table again. 'It's not a joke, I meant it.' He bent and kissed the top of her tousled head and smiled at her; he didn't look in the least tired. 'You're a jewel of a girl, Gemma—just like your name.'

He took the tray and led the way back to the sitting room and they drank the pot dry, saying very little. It was when they had finished and she was stacking the cups on the tray again that he said in a matter-of-fact voice: 'And now there is no reason why you shouldn't come back with me, is there?' He looked at her thoughtfully. 'Unless you object on personal grounds?'

Gemma cast a glance at Doctor Gibbons, who had gone to sleep and would be of no help at all. She suddenly felt very sleepy herself so that her mumbled 'No, of course I don't' was barely audible, but the professor heard all right and although his face remained placid there was a satisfied gleam in his eyes. His casual: 'Oh, good,' was uttered in tones as placid as the expression on his face, but he didn't say more than that, merely offered to escort her to her own front door, and when they reached it, advised her to go to bed at once.

A superfluous piece of advice; Gemma tore off her clothes, washed her face in a most perfunctory manner and was asleep the moment her uncombed head touched the pillow.

CHAPTER THREE

GEMMA slept all through the sounds of a household getting up and preparing itself for the day, perhaps because everyone was so much quieter than usual, for the professor, keeping watch from his window until Cousin Maud opened the back door so that Giddy might go out, presented himself at it without loss of time, and over a cup of tea with her, recounted the night's events. It was hard to believe, looking at him, that he had himself taken part in them, for he appeared the very epitome of casual elegance, freshly shaved and bathed, his blue eyes alert under their heavy lids. Only when she looked closely Maud could see the lines of fatigue in his face. A tough man, she decided as she went round the house cautioning her young relations to behave like mice so that Gemma might sleep on.

And sleep she did, until almost midday, to go downstairs much refreshed and eat an enormous meal while Cousin Maud plied her with hot coffee and questions. She ate the last of the wholesome cheese pudding before her, washed up, invited her cousin to come upstairs with her while she dressed, and signified her intention of cycling over to the ruins of Mellbury House to see exactly what was to happen. 'Perhaps it will close down for good,' she wondered worriedly. 'What do you think, Maud?'

The older woman sat down on the edge of the bed. 'Well, dear, I should think it very likely, wouldn't you? There must have been an awful lot of damage done and it would cost a fortune to re-build the place. Doctor Gibbons is coming in to tea if he can spare the time—perhaps he'll know something. He telephoned this morning—he said you were marvellous. Ross said so too.'

Gemma piled her hair neatly on top of her head and started to pin it there. 'Oh—did you see him, then?'

'He was at the back door this morning when I went down, to tell me that you'd only just got to bed.' She got up and strolled over to the window. 'You know, Gemma, it might not be such a bad idea, to take that job Ross suggested. No, don't look like that, dear—he didn't talk about it; Doctor Gibbons told me—I imagine that he thought I already knew about it.' There was faint reproach in her voice.

Gemma was making haste with her face. 'I should have told you—I did mean to, but I wasn't sure—I mean it was only to be for a week or two and although he said he could make it all right with Matron, I was a bit doubtful about her wanting me back. But now I suppose there's nothing for me to go back to.' She went and put an arm through her cousin's. 'I'll go and find out now. Would you mind if I did go? There's an awful lot to do here, you know.'

Cousin Maud, who had been doing it for years, agreed a little drily, 'But it's time Mandy and Phil helped out a little more, and you haven't had a holiday for years—not that this job sounds much like a holiday, but at least it will be a change of scene.'

Gemma mulled over her cousin's words as she cycled along the lanes and forgot them when she saw the charred ruins of the hospital. It really had been badly damaged; true, the Victorian extension at the back had escaped more or less intact, but it had never been used as wards for the patients; the rooms were poky and dark and there were any number of small staircases which the old ladies would never have managed. Gemma propped her bike against a tree and went round to the back and through a door which looked as though it belonged to a church but led instead to a narrow, damp passage leading to the back hall. It was here that Matron had her flat. Gemma knocked on the door and was relieved to hear Matron's voice bidding her go in, for she remembered then, a little late in the day, that she had gone to the Rectory. But Matron was there, all right, in uniform too, looking calm and collected, just as though the hospital hadn't been burned around her ears only a few hours earlier.

She looked up as Gemma went in and smiled at her. 'Sister Prentice, I'm glad you've come. I've been hearing about this job you've been offered—at least one of my staff won't be out of work.'

Gemma took the chair she had been waved to. 'You mean the hospital can't be rebuilt?'

Matron nodded. 'I'm almost sure of it. There's only been a preliminary survey, of course, but any idiot can see that it would need rebuilding completely—what a splendid chance for the Hospital Board, who have been wanting to close us down for months, but of course something will have to be done, the other hospitals can't absorb our old ladies permanently. At the moment they're distributed around the area, but a handful of them will be able to come to Vicar's Place—a large empty house some miles away. I don't know yet, for no one has said anything, but I hope that I shall be asked to go there as Matron until such time as larger premises can be found—probably years. I shall only need two nurses there, for it won't take more than ten patients.' She smiled at Gemma. 'It will take a very long time to settle, Sister Prentice, and I doubt if I can offer you even the prospect of a job.' She added bracingly: 'You could get a post in London very easily, you know—your references are excellent.'

Gemma shook her head. 'That wouldn't do at all, Matron. This job was marvellous, it meant that I could live at home, you see—there are so many of us and it's not fair that Cousin Maud should have to manage alone.'

Matron agreed: 'Yes, of course. Well, shall we leave things as they are and you could come and see me when you get back.'

It was a little vague, but Gemma could see that there wasn't much to be done at the moment. She agreed without demur and asked after her patients.

'Scattered round half a dozen hospitals, but unharmed, I'm glad to say. Their resilience is remarkable, isn't it? I wonder how many of them realized how near death they were—and several of them owe their lives to you and Professor Dieperink van Berhuys. We are all most grateful to you ...'

Gemma went pink. 'The professor was wonderful, but I didn't do much, Matron.' She got up. 'I'm not sure if I shall go to Holland ...' She wished she hadn't said that because Matron looked so surprised, so she added hastily: 'I'll let you know, shall I?'

It had been silly to say that, she admitted to herself as she went back home at her leisure, because of course she was sure; she was going. It would be a nice change from the old ladies, bless them. Besides, she was curious about the professor; she wanted to know exactly what work he did and where he lived and what his family was like. She wheeled her bike into the back garden and went indoors, frowning a little. She mustn't get too curious; curiosity was one thing, getting too interested was another.

The professor called round that evening, giving her an affable nod as he seated himself, at the twins' urgent request, at the kitchen table so that he might give them the benefit of his knowledge concerning the more complicated aspects of the algebra they were struggling with.

It wasn't until he had solved the knottier of the problems that he looked up to say: 'I'm returning to Holland in three days' time, Gemma—will you be coming with me?'

She glanced round her. The entire family had found its way into the kitchen by now, each of them apparently absorbed in some task which simply had to be done there, although Cousin Maud was just sitting doing nothing at all, looking at her. All of them were listening so hard for her answer that she could almost hear them doing it. She said 'yes', and then, because it had sounded rather terse: 'Thank you, Professor.'

'Thank you, Gemma,' he answered gravely, and then with an abrupt change of manner, added cheerfully: 'How about all of us gathering round the table for this?'

They had all talked at once after that; they were a united family and each member of it considered that he or she had every right to add their say to the matter. It was the professor who made sense of and produced order out of the spate of suggestions, speculations and improbable advice which was offered. Over cups of cocoa and the total disintegration of the cake which Cousin Maud had only just taken out of the oven, it was decided that Gemma should go to Salisbury in the morning to get a visitor's passport and replenish her wardrobe, but when she mentioned going to the bank to get some Dutch money, the professor pointed out that that would be quite unnecessary, for she would be paid a salary and he would advance any money she might need when they arrived in Holland.

'How much are you going to pay her?' George wanted to know, and was instantly shushed by his elders.

'Exactly the same as she receives here,' the professor told him. He looked across at Gemma. 'That is if you find that an agreeable arrangement?'

'Yes, thank you.' She tried to sound as businesslike as he did, but instead her voice sounded a little

46

ungracious, but he didn't seem to notice, only smiled a little and presently got up to go.

As he sauntered to the door he turned to say carelessly over his shoulder: 'I have business in Salisbury—I'll give you a lift. Will nine o'clock suit you?'

As soon as he had gone, Mandy made a pot of tea and they all gathered round again. Gemma hadn't been away for a holiday for a long time—true, this trip to Holland wasn't exactly that, but it was abroad, and as such, an event. Her wardrobe was discussed at length by her sisters and cousin while the boys pored over an atlas, offering occasional unhelpful advice as to what she should take with her. Her sisters had more to say, though: Gemma had nice clothes, but not—they were emphatic about that—enough. Living in a small village with not much opportunity of going out, she tended to buy serviceable, even if nice, things and make them last far too long. She was quick to take Phil's point that the professor's family might live in the middle of a town and be most frightfully fashionable, in which case she would feel quite out of things. The matter was clinched by Mandy's dreamy: 'He wears the most super clothes himself, you know, and I bet they're wildly expensive—you must have something new, Gemma darling.'

Gemma poured more tea. It was true enough, his clothes had an understated elegance which betokened money, but that didn't mean to say that he had a lot of it or that his family had either; it was a pity she didn't know. She had asked him once where

47

he lived and he had told her that he had his own home and that his parents lived within an easy distance. What was an easy distance, anyway? and he hadn't said where.

'I saw a denim jacket and skirt in Jaeger's,' she said thoughtfully, 'sand-coloured. I could get some cotton sweaters and a couple of blouses—they had some the colour of a seashell—and I suppose I'd better get another pair of slacks—there's that lovely coral pink knitted cardigan you gave me, Maud— if I got sand-coloured slacks too ... and a jersey dress ...'

'Two,' said Mandy and Phil in unison, 'and you'd better have a pretty dress for the evening.'

'I'm going as a nurse, not a house guest,' argued Gemma.

'And think how dire it would be if you met some gorgeous man who wanted to take you out and you couldn't go because you hadn't anything decent to wear.'

It didn't seem very likely; Gemma, on good terms with everyone she met, had nonetheless never been overburdened with invitations from the men of her acquaintance. And why should she? She had asked herself that question years ago and come up with the sensible answer that she was neither pretty enough nor amusing enough. She was very well liked as a kind of big sister; a confidante, because she didn't keep interrupting when they eulogized about their current girl-friends, but it had seldom entered their heads to ask her out for an evening.

She had got over the hurt of it years ago, but

deeply buried in her romantic heart was the hope that one day she might meet some man who would find her irresistible. With a reckless disregard of the amount of money she intended to spend, she said that yes, she would certainly buy something suitable for the evening. It would probably hang in the cupboard all the while she was in Holland, but there was no harm in pretending.

'Perhaps you'll wear your uniform,' suggested George suddenly, and everyone turned surprised eyes upon him.

'Never!' said Mandy hotly, but Cousin Maud looked thoughtful.

'There is that possibility,' she conceded.

Of course it was a possibility, said Gemma crossly, and why on earth hadn't she thought of it sooner? 'Probably I shall be able to get by with a new jersey dress and that cotton shirtwaister I had last summer.'

Phil groaned. 'Don't you dare! You must ask in the morning. Supposing he wants you to wear uniform, would you mind?'

Gemma shrugged. 'I'm a nurse, aren't I?' she said flatly, and added mendaciously: 'I really don't mind, you know.'

Asking the professor about it had been more difficult than she had supposed. For one thing, he talked about everything under the sun except her impending job, and it wasn't until he was threading his way through the narrow streets of Salisbury that she asked: 'Am I to wear uniform while I'm nursing your sister?'

He looked faintly surprised. 'Decidedly not; Rienieta would dislike that very much—she isn't a biddable girl.' He swung the car round a sharp corner and flashed a smile at her. 'You look—er—severe in your uniform. No, I have it wrong, that makes you sound like a gorgon and you're not that in the least—it would be better to say that it gives you an air of authority, and I'm afraid she doesn't react well to that. She's spoilt—the last of a large family, and we all dote on her.'

Gemma nodded. 'Oh, I quite understand—look at our George, he gets away with any amount of mischief ...'

The professor parked the car in the market square and sat back, in no hurry to get out. 'You see now why I am anxious that you should come back with me and look after her?' He turned to smile at her, his blue eyes twinkling. 'She's a handful, but a delightful one.'

He got out of the car and went round to open her door. 'Where shall we meet and when? Will you be free for coffee or shall we make it lunch?'

'Oh,' said Gemma ingenuously, 'I didn't know—are we going to have lunch?'

'You won't be finished before then, will you? Shall we meet at the White Hart at half past twelve? I'll wait, so don't panic if you're late.'

She agreed gravely, wondering she had ever thought of him as devious. He was nothing of the sort, he was dependable and kind, and somehow when she was with him, she didn't feel plain. She smiled up at him, suddenly happy. 'I'll get that passport first,' she told him, 'and then I must do some shopping, but I'll be there at half past twelve.'

The morning was a success. Once the business of the passport had been settled Gemma felt free to spend the money she had drawn from her account—rather more than she had intended, but she consoled herself with the thought that everything she intended buying would certainly be worn throughout the summer and probably next summer too. She arrived at the White Hart a mere ten minutes late, loaded with boxes and parcels which the professor took from her with the air of a man who had done this service many times before, before ushering her into the dining room.

They lunched with splendid appetites off cold roast beef and a great bowl of salad, and, her tongue loosened by the claret her companion had chosen and egged on by his quiet questions, Gemma talked as she hadn't talked for a long time; about her parents, who had been killed five years earlier in a car crash, and the subsequent difficulties of bringing up her brothers and sisters until Cousin Maud, coming to live with them two years back, had eased her problems. Gemma stopped rather abruptly in the middle of her paean of praise about that lady and exclaimed: 'I'm sorry, I'm talking too much.'

'No, you're not, I'm interested.' His calm voice, while allaying her fears of being a bore, made her feel that she should change the conversation, which she did rather abruptly.

'It was funny that Charlie Briggs wasn't at the fire,' she observed.

Her companion agreed. 'I take it he should have been on call and was nowhere to be found? Although from the little I saw of him I doubt if he would have been much use.'

'You're so right,' declared Gemma, her brown eyes flashing, 'and if that sounds unfair I'm sorry, but if you knew how I dislike him——' She added: 'It's strange how you dislike some people on sight.'

'And like others the moment you set eyes on them,' he offered lazily. 'I can't say I took to the young man myself. What is Matron going to do?'

They talked about the hospital for a few minutes until the professor suggested that they might finish their shopping together. 'I should like to get your cousin something. She's been very kind—cups of tea and cake ...' He smiled his pleasant smile. 'What do you suggest?'

They spent another hour or so at the shops and it was only much later, sitting quietly with Maud when the others had gone to bed, that Gemma remembered that she hadn't asked the professor a single question about his home or his family.

And two days later, sitting beside him as they drove away from the village, she wondered if she would wake up suddenly and find that everything had been a dream. The few days had flashed by, she had tried on all her new clothes for the edification of her brothers and sisters, packed them neatly and then gone about her usual household chores, and during that time she had barely exchanged a couple of words with the professor. He had told her, on their way back from Salisbury, at what time they would be leaving and apparently had seen no need to remind her of it. She had eaten a hurried breakfast in the bosom of her family and had then been escorted to the front gate by all of them, to find the professor already there, leaning on his car's elegant bonnet, so that her goodbyes had been swift before he had packed her tidily into the seat beside his, disposed of her luggage in the boot, said his own goodbyes with cheerful brevity, and driven off. Now they were already through Salisbury and he had put his large, well shod foot down on the accelerator and kept it there. He was a fast driver but a careful one, taking traffic jams and the like with a massive calm which made light of them.

They were crossing from Dover by Hovercraft and driving up through France and Belgium. Bergen-op-Zoom, Gemma had discovered, was their destination, and now she was studying the map to discover just where that was.

The professor had elected to go via Andover and pick up the M3 beyond that town, which meant that he could keep up a good seventy miles an hour until they reached Chobham, where he turned off for Dorking and a cross-country route. They stopped at Seal for coffee and then presently picked up the M2 and finally the A2 into Dover. It had been a pleasant run, Gemma conceded to herself. Either the professor knew the route very well indeed or he had an excellent bump of locality, for he hadn't once evinced uncertainty as to their road, nor had he shown any sign of irritation at the small delays they had had, and he had kept up an entertaining flow of small talk which had passed the time very agreeably. Gemma, pleased with her world, stepped on board the Hovercraft and was whisked towards the coast of France. If there was a fly in her ointment it was a very small one; the professor, she was well aware, was a relaxed man by nature, but did he need to relax so completely that he should fall asleep and stay so, peacefully, for the entire crossing, and leaving her to her own devices? True, he had provided her with magazines and a refreshing drink, but it was the kind of behaviour one might expect from a husband ... Perhaps she should take it as a compliment that he should stand on so little ceremony with her. She stared out, watching the coast of France coming closer with every second, and when she looked at him again it was to find him watching her.

He smiled at once as she caught his eye and said apologetically: 'So sorry—shocking manners, I'm afraid.' He was wide awake now. 'I didn't have much sleep last night—Mrs Turner's twins ...'

Her eyes opened wide. 'They never arrived—why, Doctor Gibbons said they weren't due ...'

'And nor were they; they stole a march on us and he was out at Giles Farm.'

'Oh, so you delivered them.' She was full of concern. 'You must be dog-tired. Couldn't we pull in somewhere after we land so that you could have another nap?'

'How accommodating of you, dear girl, but there's no need of that. I feel in splendid shape.

54

We'll have a meal, though.'

An invitation to which Gemma readily agreed, for she was famished.

So presently, half an hour's drive from Calais, they stopped to eat enormous omelettes at a road-side café; they polished off a bowl of salad too and drank several cups of coffee before, much refreshed, they took to the road once more. They had turned away from the coast now, cutting across the country to pick up the motorway to Ghent and then on to Antwerp. The professor skirted the city, but all the same, the traffic slowed them up a little so that Gemma was relieved to hear him say: 'I'm sure you're dying for a cup of tea. We're not far from the frontier now, so we'll stop in Holland—there's a roadhouse just on the other side of the *douanes*.'

The tea came in glasses and without milk, but it was refreshing, and Gemma drank it thankfully. She looked as fresh and tidy as when they had set out that morning; her neat coil of hair was still pinned on top of her head, her blue and white jersey dress had no creases, she looked cool and composed even though she felt neither. They had only another twenty or so miles to go and she was beginning to wonder what her patient would be like, whether she would like her, whether his family would mind her coming ... She said suddenly: 'Does your mother know I'm coming? I mean, I know I'm supposed to be a surprise, but surely only to Rienieta?'

She looked at him so anxiously that he sat up in his chair and said reassuringly: 'My parents know that you are coming and very much approve of the idea—did I not tell you?' And when she shook her head: 'I'm sorry about that, but I can assure you that you will be most warmly welcomed.' He gave her a quick nod and added, 'You're worrying—don't!'

They were back in the car now, tearing down the motorway, and presently he said: 'We're just coming in to the outskirts of the town—see that mediaeval gate ahead of us? We go through there.'

Gemma looked about her; they were passing pleasant villas, each set in its own neat garden bright with flowers, and very shortly these became terraced houses with a shop here and there, and rising above them, the magnificent gateway; it led to the heart of the town through a narrow winding street of more shops and which in its turn opened out on to a square lined with old houses, a hotel or two, a great church and a splendid town hall, but she was given no time to see much of these, for the professor kept straight on across the square and into another narrow street going slightly uphill, leading away from the town again.

'You shall explore some time,' he promised her. 'My parents live a mile or two away. We're on the road to Breda now, but we turn off presently; they live on the edge of a small village.'

The country was so flat that Gemma could see its houses when he pointed them out to her, and at that distance they appeared a mere huddle of tiled roofs dominated by two towering churches.

'Two?' asked Gemma.

'Protestant and Roman Catholic.'

'But it's such a very small village . . .'

'But a wide-flung parish—besides, everyone goes to church in these parts.'

She gave him a quick look. 'I never thought to ask—I mean, if you're R.C. I'm not.'

'My dear girl, my family has been stubbornly Protestant for some hundreds of years—and once upon a time it wasn't easy to be that—the Spanish Occupation, you know. But now we all get on well together although you will find separate schools and clubs—hospitals too.'

'Isn't that rather limiting?'

'Not really,' he grinned briefly. 'The talent seems to be fairly evenly distributed on both sides.'

The village was quaint, with a minute square across which the two churches faced each other, flanked by a café, the tiny Gemeentehuis, one or two shops and a row of very small houses. But they didn't stop here either, but took a cobbled road past one of the churches which ran into the open country again. There was a canal now, the evening light reflected in its quiet water, and the road looked as though it led to nowhere. But it did; a very small signpost pointed the way in important letters to Breda—a back way, explained the professor, which cut off quite a few miles if one knew the way well enough. 'And here we are,' he exclaimed as they passed a copse and came round a curve in the road which disclosed a white-painted, square house set in a fair sized garden. There were iron railings all round and a glimpse of outbuildings and wilder ground at the side. The professor drove through the wide open gates and drove up the straight drive to the front door where he alighted before helping Gemma out. She stood for a moment, her hand still in his, looking at the house; it had a plain face, a solid door under a weighty porch and precise rows of large square windows showing only a glimpse of curtains. For lack of a word, she described it to herself as well established.

'Like it?' asked her companion.

'Oh, yes—yes, very much.' She stopped as the door was opened and a short, fat man held it wide. 'Ah,' said the professor, 'here is Ignaas.' And at her look of inquiry: 'He's been with us for so long that I can't remember when he wasn't here.'

He was still holding her hand in his, just as if he knew that she was nervous; perhaps Ignaas guessed it too, for his round face broke into a smile as Gemma bade him how do you do, and as for the professor, he clapped the older man on the back and made some laughing remark which changed the smile into a deep, rich chuckle as they were led into the hall, a square apartment with a polished wood floor, crimson wall hangings and some extremely solid oak furniture. Very old, thought Gemma, craning her neck stealthily as they went.

They were shown into a room at the side of the hall through massive mahogany double doors crowned by an abundance of carved and gilded woodwork. It was large and lofty and furnished with a nice assortment of richly covered easy chairs, occasional tables, display cabinets and an enormous carved pillow cupboard which took up half one wall. The windows were wide and high and curtained with swathes of crimson brocade and the white walls were hung with a vast collection of paintings, mostly portraits. Gemma's mouth hung open slightly at the sight of so much richness; it reminded her of some stately home or other she had once visited. She had never imagined that people actually lived their day-to-day lives surrounded by such treasures, but apparently they did, for there was a small boy sitting on the carpet in the centre of the room, the bricks he was playing with in tumbled heaps around him, and there was a slightly older girl sharing one of the great chairs with a corgi dog. There was a pile of knitting thrown down carelessly on one of the velvet-upholstered sofas and a young woman lying full length on the floor, her chin in her hand, reading. They all looked up at the same time and made a concerted dash for the professor, who received their onslaught with great good humour, tossing the children into the air before bending to kiss the girl.

'Gemma, this is my elder sister Gustafina and her two children—Bessel and Wijanda—we call her Nanda.' And when she had shaken hands with them all: 'You're staying?' he asked his sister, 'or is this a brief visit?'

They were alike, Gemma could see that watching them together, although Gustafina was quite a lot younger; they had the same handsome good looks and bright blue eyes, and so, for that matter, had the two children. The pair of them grinned at her shyly and their mother said: 'They like you, I think—we shall come again so that they may make friends.'

The professor offered Gemma a chair and asked idly; 'You're not staying for the evening?' His blue eyes were amused. 'Curious, Gustafina?' And when she smiled: 'Where is Mama?'

'Upstairs with Rienieta—she has been difficult.' She smiled at Gemma. 'We are all so glad that you could come, for she is not a good patient and my mother finds it so difficult to be firm with her when she is ill . . .' She broke off. 'There is Piet, I can hear the car. We have to go.'

The man who entered the room was quite unlike the husband Gemma had expected. He was short and thickset and not in the least good-looking, although he had a pleasant face. He was a good deal older than Gustafina, who quite obviously adored him, and it was also obvious that he was on very good terms with the professor. 'We are delighted,' he told her when he was introduced, 'and we shall hope to see more of you—we live only a short distance away, and when you find Rienieta is too much for you then you must escape to us.'

Everyone laughed and Gemma, laughing with them, knew that she was going to like being with these people. Never mind if her patient was difficult, everyone else was super; that nice old man who had opened the door, the professor's sister and the children, and now this cheerful little man . . . The only thing which worried her now was meeting Rienieta's mother and father.

Her mother walked in at that very moment, just

as though she had answered a cue in a play, and Gemma was surprised once more, for Mevrouw Dieperink van Berhuys wasn't at all what she had expected; she was short and cosily plump, with a round face, dark eyes and silver hair drawn back in a simple knot. She was wearing a soft blue dress, cut so skilfully that one forgot, looking at her, how plump she was.

She beamed at everyone in general as she came in, but it was to the professor she went first, and he went to meet her, giving her a great hug before saying over his shoulder: 'Gemma, come here and meet my mother.'

There had been no need to worry, Gemma realized; this dear little lady wasn't frightening at all. She broke at once into apologies for not being there to welcome them and then went on to ask a great many questions about their trip. 'You're in Holland for the first time?' she asked Gemma. 'You shall see something of it while you are with us and we are so very glad to have you. It is unkind to say so, but I am so very glad that there was a fire at your hospital, otherwise you would not have come.' She added hastily, 'Not that I would wish any harm to come to your patients, it must have been dreadful for them. I think that I would rather die than be pushed down one of those chutes.' She smiled charmingly. 'Ross told me.'

Gemma smiled in reply. 'They're awful,' she admitted, 'and I was terrified.' After a little pause she asked: 'Would you like me to go to my patient now?'

61

The dark eyes twinkled at her; the little lady wasn't in the least like her son—or her daughter for that matter, but there was something about her which reminded Gemma forcibly of the professor; probably the smile, she concluded. 'My dear child, first you shall have a drink with us and we can tell you a little about Rienieta and talk about your free time and such things, for they are important, are they not?' Her face suddenly softened and glowed. 'Here is my husband.'

A tall man in his late sixties had come into the room, kissed his grandchildren and his daughter, exchanged a few words with the professor and Piet and come to join his wife. He was a handsome man still; it was easy to see where the professor and his sister got their good looks. His voice was as deep and slow as his son's. 'Ah, our nurse from England—we are pleased to welcome you to our home, my dear. Ross took care of you on the journey?'

The two men smiled at each other and the woman between them beamed at them both and said to Gemma: 'There are more of us for you to meet, but you have brothers and sisters, too, have you not, so you will not feel nervous. Now we will sit down and drink a glass of sherry and then I will take you to see Rienieta.'

A delightful family circle, thought Gemma, sipping from delicate crystal; the children sprawled on their father's knee while the rest of them chatted, always in English, about nothing in particular. The effect was so soothing that she could have fallen asleep, and when the professor caught her eye and smiled she smiled back warmly; he was a nice man, so of course he would have a nice family—they were a bit like her own, actually, close-knit and friendly and yet casual. She wondered what they were all doing at home and glanced at the handsome gilt clock on the chimneypiece. The professor saw the look and crossed the room to sit beside her and murmur: 'Having supper, I expect, don't you? You shall telephone them presently.'

'Oh, may I? That would be super.' She looked at him thoughtfully. 'How did you know I was thinking about them?'

'Your face is easy to read.'

She couldn't think of anything to say to that, so instead she asked: 'Should I go to Rienieta now?'

'If you're ready. My sister and her husband are going presently, but Mama will take you upstairs.' He got up and Gemma got up too, said her goodbyes and followed his mother from the room, across the hall and up the stairs, looking around her as she went. In the gallery which ran round three sides of the hall, her hostess paused. 'Rienieta is our youngest,' she explained, 'and a darling child, but somehow this wretched fever has made her feel bad, but I thing that she will like you and you must understand that we shall not interfere with you in any way. She needs a firm hand and Ross is quite sure that you will know exactly how best to go about getting her well again.' She walked on, past several doors, and turned down a short corridor. 'This is her room, and yours is next to it, with a bathroom on the other side, and I hope you will feel at home, Gemma. And now I think I will go in with you and then leave you for a little while.' She put out a pretty, beringed hand to open the door.

CHAPTER FOUR

But it wasn't Mevrouw Dieperink van Berhuys who opened the door after all; the professor came leaping up the staircase to join them, remarking as he did so: 'It doesn't seem quite fair to leave the introductions to you, Mama—I'll take Gemma in.'

He held the door open as he spoke and she felt herself propelled by a firm hand in the small of her back, into the room—a charming apartment, all pale colours and dainty furniture, the carpet inches thick under her feet. There were a great many china trifles scattered around and some exquisite silver, and the bed was an enchanting affair with a frilled muslin canopy tied with pink ribbons. Its occupant's hair was tied with pink ribbons too—a very pretty girl whose prettiness just now was marred by a heavy frown. She spoke in Dutch and crossly, glaring at her brother from bright blue eyes.

He answered her in English. 'Hullo, Rienieta, and don't glower at me like that, *lieveling*—you know that I've been in England and couldn't come to see you before.' He crossed the room and dropped a kiss on top of her head. 'But I know all about you being ill—besides, I telephoned you, so don't look so cross, you spoilt brat.' He tugged gently at a blonde curl. 'I've brought you a present, and better than that, I've brought Gemma with me.'

'Who's she?' demanded the petulant young lady in the bed. She eyed Gemma warily.

'A friend of mine—she lives next door to Doctor Gibbons, and I teased her and tormented her to come back with me and keep you company until you're well.' He drew Gemma to the bed and took her hand in his. 'Gemma, this is Rienieta, feeling very sorry for herself just at present, but you'll know how to deal with that, I've no doubt.'

'A nurse,' stated his sister in a frigid voice which barely concealed her opinion of the profession.

'And a very good one. Gemma comes from a large family too—she's the eldest.'

Rienieta took another look at Gemma. 'How many brothers and sisters have you?' she wanted to know.

'Five—the youngest is ten years old.'

'I'm seventeen—Ross is very old, he's thirty-seven, almost thirty-eight.'

'Yes, he told me,' said Gemma placidly. 'I'm twenty-five, but I haven't had a chance to get old yet, the family don't give me a chance.'

Her patient smiled. 'I think I shall like you,' she decided. 'I'm sorry if I was rude, but the nurse I had was quite old and so strict and she never laughed. She had no brothers and sisters and didn't like children.'

'Poor thing,' said Gemma with sincere pity. 'It's fun being one of a large family, isn't it?'

'Yes—are you very strict too?'

Gemma considered. 'No, I don't think I am, but

I'm not all that easy-going either.' Her plain face was lightened by a wide smile. 'The others do what I tell them, anyway.'

'Oh, well, I suppose I shall too. Do you play cards?'

'Like an expert—it's our favourite pastime during the winter evenings—cribbage too, and draughts and dominoes and very bad chess. Do you?'

Rienieta nodded happily. 'That is good news, for when I feel well we can play, can we not?' She turned a much more cheerful face to the professor, who had been leaning nonchalantly against the foot of the bed, not saying a word. 'You are a dear kind brother, Ross, to bring me this so nice Gemma. I shall now get well very quickly.'

He grinned down at her. 'Well, my dear, that's a good start, but remember that it's a slow business; you're allergic to all the antibiotics which would cure you in a few days, so we shall have to go to the long way round—but it won't be all that long if you do as Gemma says.' He bent to kiss her again. 'I must be on my way, I've been idle far too long. *Tot ziens.*' He nodded with casual friendliness to Gemma, murmured that his mother would be back and went out of the room, shutting the door silently behind him.

'Ross is my favourite brother,' confided Rienieta. 'He is a little large perhaps, but he is kind and amusing and almost never cross, though he has a truly dreadful temper, you know—so have I,' she added rather unnecessarily. 'He is also very handsome. You like him too?'

'He's very nice,' said Gemma sedately. 'Now tell me what you do all day and perhaps we can make bed more bearable—have you been getting up at all?'

They spent the next ten minutes discussing Rienieta's feelings on the subject of being ill and being thwarted—one would imagine most cruelly—by her parents from doing what she wanted to do and not what the doctor wished. 'And there are puppies in the stable,' she finished, 'and Mama will not let me go and see them ...'

'I should think not indeed!' said Gemma in the severe tones she used to remonstrate with George. 'You see, while you have a high temperature you just have to stay quiet, but I don't see why I couldn't bring them to see you one day soon—we'll ask your parents, anyway. Once your fever has gone you'll feel better and your joints won't ache either, and then I daresay the doctor will let you go downstairs for a little while.' She got up and went to look out of the window at the pretty garden below. 'What sort of puppies are they?'

They were happily absorbed in this interesting subject when Rienieta's mother came back again, and Gemma got up once more to go with her. So far, so good, she thought, and followed Mevrouw Dieperink van Berhuys out of the room.

It seemed to her that her own room was just as beautiful as that of her patient. True, there was no canopy over the bed, which was a narrow one of the Second Empire style, but its coverlet was of thick silk lavishly embroidered with flowers, and the carpeted floor was just as cosy to her feet, and over and above the highly polished dressing table and tallboy and little bedside table, there was a small armchair drawn up to the window, with a table beside it piled high with English magazines and books. Gemma eyed it all appreciatively—even if her patient turned out to be the most difficult she had ever had, there would be compensations.

And thinking over her evening as she lay in bed later, too excited to sleep, she didn't think that Rienieta would be too difficult. She was spoilt, but then so, in a way, was her brother George—the last of a long family could expect indulgence. It was apparent that the professor's family were comfortably off, perhaps more than that; Gemma, who had never been comfortably off in her life, sighed over the wealth of silver and crystal and hand-painted china which had decked the dining table. She sighed, too, at the memory of the delicious food she had eaten and registered a resolve there and then not to eat too much—she was already, in her own eyes, on the plump side.

She had liked the head of the family too and the professor's younger brother, Bart, home for the evening, and another sister, Hendrina, whom everyone called Iny. She was almost as pretty as Gustafina and a good deal quieter. Gemma had liked her immediately and had been disappointed to find that she didn't live at home; she was training to be a nurse in Utrecht and had only come home, like Bart, to meet Gemma. When she had wished her goodbye she had said: 'Ross was quite right, you're

69

just the person Rienieta needs. He said you were sensible—a no-nonsense girl, who didn't flutter her eyelashes every time he opened his mouth.'

Gemma had been unable to think of anything to say to that, although she had been conscious of annoyance at his opinion of her. She turned over now in her comfortable bed and thought inconsequently that her eyelashes were about the only thing worth looking at in her face—long and brown and curling. The professor couldn't have noticed.

She saw neither hair nor hide of the professor during the next three days, not that she would have had a moment to spare for him if she had; Rienieta's fever had returned, persistent and high, leaving her miserable and ill and extremely bad-tempered. Gemma, caring for her with all the skill at her command, went short of sleep and took almost no time off at all, reassuring the various members of the family who worried about this that she would take extra time off later on. Rienieta wasn't going to die, she wasn't seriously ill, but the very nature of her illness made her disagreeable, especially with her family, who became quite upset, but Gemma, used to dealing with fractious patients, allowed the mutterings and lowered brow to pass unnoticed while she concentrated on getting the invalid better.

It was hard on the girl, of course, for if she hadn't been allergic to antibiotics, she would have been cured by now, whereas the more conservative treatment she was having required patience, and she had very little of that. It was tiring work, but it wouldn't last for ever, as Gemma kept reassuring her patient's mother, whose pleasant round face was puckered with worry. She reassured herself as well, thinking wistfully that it would be nice to have a few hours off and see something of the quiet countryside around them.

Rienieta's mother had been kindness itself, showing Gemma the house in a snatched half hour, showing her the grounds surrounding it, making sure that she had everything for her comfort. Gemma was tempted on one or two occasions to ask about the professor; no one—in her hearing, at any rate—had mentioned him, and it seemed strange that he hadn't come to see the little sister of whom he was so fond. Possibly he had telephoned, though, and if he had, there could be no reason for telling her.

Gemma retired to bed on the third evening quite worn out, for Rienieta had been more difficult than usual during the day, although she had seemed a little better when Gemma had settled her down for the night; indeed, creeping into her room just before she got into her own bed, she was relieved to find her patient asleep. She went back to her own room and lost no time in following her example.

She was roused an hour or two later, though; the little electric bell by her bed saw to that. As she padded to Rienieta's room she heard the great wall clock in the hall below chime one o'clock and yawned as she slid silently through the half open door.

'I can't sleep,' said Rienieta pettishly. 'I'm hot and I've been awake for hours.' She added with charming inconsequence: 'How pretty you look with your hair hanging down your back.'

Gemma held back another yawn. 'It's this flattering light, it's pretty enough to make even me passable by it. Shall I sponge your face and hands, love? And then a drink, perhaps? How about a cup of tea?'

Rienieta had cheered up a little. 'The English drink much tea, but I will drink a cup of it to please you.'

'Good, and I'll have one with you—there's something rather special about drinking tea in the middle of the night while everyone else is asleep.' Gemma was bustling gently about the room. 'Face and hands first.'

She was deft and quick and still managed to give the impression that time was of no consequence to her at all. She combed Rienieta's damp hair, shook up her pillows and switched on another little pink lamp.

'I'll be five minutes,' she promised, and stole away, down the stairs and across the hall with its dim wall lights, and through the arched door which led to the kitchens, the main one of which was a vast, old-fashioned place with its scrubbed table and high-backed chairs on each side of the Aga stove. There was plenty of up-to-date equipment too; Gemma put on the electric kettle and went to the enormous cupboard which filled the whole of one wall, in search of tea.

'It's on the second shelf, on the left,' advised the professor from the dimness behind her, and she shot round to stare a little wildly, uttering a small squeak of fright as she did so. 'Well, really!' she said, and her voice was a little loud and high. 'Frightening me like that in the dead of night—and how did you get in, anyway?'

'I have a key,' he told her mildly. 'I was in the pantry looking for something to eat.'

She reached for the tea, took it over to the teapot and carefully warmed the pot before spooning it in. Only then did she ask: 'Haven't you had any supper?'

He shook his head. 'I've been in Vienna. Father telephoned me about Rienieta, but I was unable to get away. I drove straight here as soon as I could—I shall spend the night here, Mama keeps a room ready for me, you know.' He walked towards her. 'How is Rienieta?'

He was lounging at the pantry door, watching her, and Gemma was suddenly aware of her hastily tugged on dressing gown and dishevelled hair, so that she spoke more sharply than she had intended, feeling shy. 'She's not been well at all, but I think she's a little better—she couldn't sleep, so I came down to make tea.'

'Splendid—may I join the party? And a little buttered toast, perhaps?' He sounded hopeful and vaguely wistful so that she forgot about her untidy appearance and said in a soothing voice: 'Why, of course—and how about a couple of boiled eggs?'

He brightened visibly. 'How kind—there's a ham here, I'll carve a slice or two.' He paused as he turned away. 'You, too?'

'No, thanks,' said Gemma politely; a cup of tea would be nice, but to devour ham and eggs at half past one in the morning between bouts of sleep sounded like indigestion to her. Possibly the professor was made of sterner stuff.

He undoubtedly was; he devoured a huge meal, perched on the side of his sister's bed, entertaining her with a lighthearted account of his three days in Vienna. He was really rather clever, thought Gemma, studying him covertly from the chair into which she had curled herself. Rienieta was happy again; she looked hot and weary still but already she looked drowsy too. The professor's voice, keeping up a quiet monologue, was very soothing. Gemma resisted a strong desire to shut her own eyes and began, very quietly, to tidy the cups and saucers back on to the tray. Then she gently tucked her patient in once more and with a look at the professor intended to warn him not to stay too long, she trod downstairs bearing the tray. The clock chimed two resonant notes as she went and she yawned again. A whole hour of her much-needed beauty sleep gone, but it had been rather fun. Somehow the professor made life more interesting ... she heard him on the staircase behind her and as he took the tray from her grasp, he said: 'I'll help you wash up ...'

But in the kitchen he put the tray down on the table and left it there. 'Ria or Nel will do something about it in the morning,' he assured her, and with one quick, unexpected movement, lifted her to sit on the table beside the tray and then got up beside her. 'Tell me about Rienieta,' he begged. 'Father telephoned me each day and I spoke to Doctor Kasten, but it's your opinion I want—you see her all day and every day ...' He glanced sideways at her. 'Probably you've been seeing too much of her?'

Gemma brushed the hair out of her eyes and shook her head. 'Oh, no—she's a dear girl, you know, and she can't help being depressed—you're as aware of that as I am. She's had a very trying time and quite a lot of pain, but I think she's over the worst of it—this is the third recurrence, isn't it? I hope it will be the last—she's strong and young and very fit usually, isn't she? For what it's worth I'd say she was on the mend.'

He flung a careless arm round her shoulders. 'And I think you're right. She may have another bout, but less severe. I'll have another talk to Kasten and see if he'll consider letting her do more—she needs concrete evidence that she's getting better, don't you agree? He's a good man, but old-fashioned.' She felt his arm tighten a little. 'And you? You're happy? You've had no time to yourself, have you—we'll make up for that, though.'

'Well, I don't know what I'd do with it if I had it,' remarked Gemma practically, 'though your mother said that I might borrow a bike and explore a bit.'

He was staring at his feet, his head bent. 'You're content with very little, Gemma.'

'Me? Am I?' She considered. 'Not really, but if you haven't had something you don't hanker after it, do you?' She added in a matter-of-fact way: 'I think you have everything.'

He said at his mildest: 'No—there is just one thing I hanker for.' He paused and she longed to know what it was, but managed not to ask. She said instead: 'I expect you'll get it.'

'Er—yes, I have that intention,' and he asked to surprise her: 'Have you a boy-friend, Gemma?'

'Me? Heavens, no!' She was quite astonished. 'I've never had the time,' she told him simply, 'although that must sound silly—and I'm not pretty.'

He said very quietly: 'My mother isn't pretty, but my father considers her to be quite beautiful, so do we all—and my grandmother had a cast in one eye and a little beaky nose, and my grandfather was her devoted slave.'

Gemma wriggled a bit. 'Well, they must have had something ... your mother is charming. I expect charm has something to do with it.' She heard with astonishment the clock strike the half hour. 'Look, I must go to bed, and so should you. Do you have to work tomorrow?'

He got off the table and scooped her down to stand beside him. 'Yes, but not until the early afternoon.' His hand on her shoulder propelled her towards the door, where he turned the light out. 'How are your family?'

His hand felt friendly. 'They're fine—your mother allows me to telephone home, you know. George has broken Doctor Gibbons' window again.'

The professor chuckled. 'He'll grow out of it,' he told her comfortably as they went up the wide stairs. In the long dimly lit gallery which encircled the hall below he patted her shoulder in avuncular fashion, dropped a casual kiss on to the top of her head, and wished her goodnight. Gemma murmured sleepily and padded down the passage to her room, peeping in at Rienieta on the way; she was fast asleep. Gemma, on the point of entering her own room, looked back. The professor was still standing in the gallery. She waved briefly before she closed her door. He really was rather a dear.

He wasn't at breakfast in the morning. Gemma, having seen to her patient's wants, shared her meal with the lady of the house and no one else. Bart had gone back to medical school and Iny was at the hospital. Klaas, older than Bart, she hadn't met yet; he was married and living in Friesland. She glanced round the empty table and as though she had read her thoughts, Mevrouw Dieperink van Berhuys remarked: 'Just the two of us, my dear; my husband and Ross went out early. Ross has to go back to Utrecht shortly, although I daresay he will go and see Rienieta before he goes.'

'He saw her last night,' said Gemma, and unaware that her hostess knew all about it already, recounted the night's activities, vaguely put out because the professor wasn't at the breakfast table and just as vaguely glad that she would see him before he went away again.

Only she didn't. When she got back to Rienieta's room it was to find that he had already said goodbye to her and was on the point of leaving the house. Indeed, she heard the powerful roar of his car not five minutes later. For some reason she felt put out, although she concealed her feelings well enough, telling herself that she was doubtless tired.

Doctor Kasten came later in the day and pronounced himself satisfied that Rienieta had recovered from her relapse. 'The spleen is no longer enlarged,' he told Gemma, 'and the joints much less painful, although we must do another agglutination test tomorrow. Perhaps a little distraction, eh, Nurse? Shall we allow the patient to go down for an hour or so this afternoon—with all precautions, of course?'

Gemma agreed, although she had a shrewd suspicion that Rienieta, given an inch, would take an ell if she were given half a chance, and be back in bed again in no time at all. She repaired to the sickroom and delivered a homily on the subject of doing too much too soon, very much in the manner of an elder sister, and surprisingly her patient listened to her patiently and promised to do exactly as she was told.

So the day passed very satisfactorily, with Rienieta going down for her tea, dressed in her most becoming dressing gown and with her hair carefully arranged. She ate a good tea, too, surrounded by those members of her family who happened to be home for the occasion—but not the professor. Gemma, sitting a little apart from the family circle, regretted that.

Tea was almost over when there was a bustle in the hall and Bart came in and with him a young man of Gemma's age—a slim, good-looking man with dark hair worn rather long, and even though he wasn't above middle height he commanded

78

attention, perhaps because of the elegance of his clothes—not the subdued elegance and conservative cut of the professor, but trendy and wildly expensive. He stood in the doorway, smiling with charm at everyone there, and the younger members of the party greeted him with cries of 'Leo!' and a gabble of swift talk, although the professor's parents, while greeting him with courtesy, displayed no great pleasure at seeing him. But he was, of course, invited to sit down and have a cup of tea from the fresh pot Ignaas had brought in, and he was on the point of doing this when his eyes lighted upon Gemma.

He got up again at once, crying in English: 'But no one has introduced us—it is Rienieta's nurse, is it not? I have heard of her from Bart.'

Gemma shook hands and murmured, feeling, for some reason, shy—perhaps because this young man eyed her with the kind of look she wasn't used to receiving. It was absurd, but he somehow conveyed the idea that he found her enchanting and pretty and exquisitely dressed, and all this while making the most commonplace remarks. She answered him sedately enough, aware that the new dress she was wearing was really the only pretty thing about her, but he didn't appear to notice her cool manner, but engaged her in conversation for some minutes before going over to sit with Rienieta on the big sofa by the window. It was later, when she was ushering her patient back upstairs, that he followed them into the hall on the pretext of speaking to Rienieta. Whatever it was he wanted to say only took a moment, though, and as she went on up the staircase he put out a retaining hand to stop Gemma following her. 'We must see more of each other,' he said, soft-voiced, 'when are you free?'

'I really don't know.' She wished she did with all her heart, and that same heart doubled its beat when he went on: 'I'll telephone you—I want to take you out.'

She smiled a little, wished him goodbye and ran up the stairs after Rienieta, who was loitering along very slowly indeed, and when they reached her room she turned an impish face to Gemma. 'I was listening,' she declared. 'You ought to be careful of Leo, he's a—lady-killer—is that the word?'

'That's the word,' said Gemma crisply, 'and I don't quite see what I have to be careful about, do you?'

Her patient gave her a thoughtful look. 'No, you don't see, do you? Oh, well, never mind—I'm only teasing. He's fun, isn't he?'

Gemma was turning down the bed and plumping up the pillows. 'Well, I really haven't had a chance to find out,' she confessed. 'Now sit down, love, while I take your temperature—if it's O.K. we'll have a game of cards before you get ready for bed, if you would like that.'

The temperature was fine; the two of them played beggar-my-neighbour for the next hour and then with the small, numerous evening chores to keep her busy, Gemma thought no more of Leo. She thought about him later, though, when she was in bed. He had been mentioned several times during dinner that evening and she had been able to piece something of his life together. He had known the family for years; his people lived only a few miles away, he did nothing to earn his living. She rather gathered from what the head of the household said that he disapproved of that—he had money, more than enough, but that, according to old Doctor Dieperink van Berhuys, was no reason to be idle. He was engaged to be married, too—to some girl no one had ever seen who lived in Curaçao, so that no one took the engagement very seriously, least of all Leo. Gemma had had the feeling that he wasn't really approved of, although the younger ones had voted him great fun and very amusing. She found herself thinking about him for quite some time, and on the edge of sleep at last, she admitted to herself that the professor, although a perfect dear, lacked the excitement the afternoon's visitor had engendered in her.

He occupied rather too much of her thoughts during the next day too. It was only at the end of that day that she allowed herself to admit to disappointment—she had actually believed him when he had said that he wanted to see her again. She was, she told herself, getting soft in the head. With great difficulty she made herself think about something else, and went to sleep.

Leo telephoned the next day in the middle of lunch, so that Ignaas, serving the meal and going to answer the telephone, had first to tell Mevrouw Dieperink van Berhuys that the call was for Gemma from Mijnheer de Vos. He stood impassive while

81

the information was translated for Gemma's benefit, but as she made her excuses and left the table she caught him looking at her with a kind of fatherly concern. She liked Ignaas, but she had no time to think about him now. She picked up the receiver, aware of excitement, which was why her voice came out rather coldly in a bald 'Hullo.'

'Oh, she's cross,' said Leo's soft voice. 'Are they working you too hard? Ross is a slave-driver ...'

Gemma wouldn't have that. 'He's not—he's kind and considerate and clever ...'

'And dull ... I sometimes wonder if he has ever kissed a girl—his work is his life.' And then, as though he sensed that he had offended her, he went on: 'He's a very clever man and highly esteemed in his world and I expect he's kissed dozens of girls. Am I forgiven?'

Gemma smiled at the telephone. 'Yes, of course, only please remember that I admire the professor very much.'

'So do we all, darling. Are you free this evening?'

'Well, I'm not sure—I suppose I could be if I asked. I haven't had much time off so far, and Rienieta is better. I could leave her for an hour or so, I expect.'

He sounded amused. 'Good. I'll take you out to dine and dance.'

'Won't that make it a bit late?'

'If I promise to bring you back on the stroke of midnight?'

'Well, all right—but you'll have to wait while I ask ...'

82

Of course no one raised any objection, only her hostess looked faintly uneasy about it. But Gemma, on top of her little world, didn't notice that. She promised to be ready at eight o'clock and went back to finish her lunch, and beyond a few polite comments on her chance to see a little of the social life outside the house, no one said anything.

A surprisingly acquiescent Rienieta made no bones about being readied for bed earlier than usual; Gemma had time to put on the pink crêpe dress her sisters had insisted that she should buy. Had they not said, half jokingly that she had to have a pretty dress just in case she met some gorgeous man? And she had. She took great pains with her plain little face, arranged her hair in its usual top-knot and went downstairs a few minutes early. Mandy and Phil would have been shocked at that; they both believed in keeping a man waiting, but Gemma, unversed in female wiles, didn't dare. She reached the last tread of the stair as the big door opened from outside and the professor came in. He closed it without haste, looking at her. 'Very nice,' he said at length. 'Who's the lucky man?'

'Leo de Vos. He—he's taking me out for an hour or two.' She thought for a moment that he frowned, but the light in the hall was dim and when she looked more closely he was smiling faintly as he so often did. All the same she went on quite unnecessarily: 'I met him when he came here the other day with Bart.'

The smile was still there, but he offered no comment, so she went on a little faster: 'I don't expect you know that Rienieta came down to tea the day before yesterday, and she's been down each day since. Doctor Kasten is very pleased with her.' She moved a little uneasily because his silence bothered her. 'If you would rather that I stayed with her, I will—I don't mind a bit . . .'

'My dear Gemma,' he sounded very amused, 'of course you mind. Leo is a most amusing companion. I have no doubt that you will have a delightful evening.' She thought he was going to say something else, but he lapsed into silence to break it presently with: 'Have a nice time. I'm going up to see Rienieta.'

He crossed the hall and went past her and up the staircase, taking the broad, shallow steps two at a time. Gemma had the odd sensation that she had been deprived of something, although she had no idea what it might be—it was a vague, half-felt feeling and instantly dispelled by the imperious blast of a horn outside. Leo, for her, presumably.

The professor had been quite right; Leo was an amusing companion, and Gemma, simple in such matters, took his subtle compliments as gospel truth, and his sly innuendoes for the most part passed over her head. She saw no point in pretending that she wasn't enjoying herself, because she was, very much —Leo had taken care of that; he had chosen to take her to the Princeville, a smart restaurant just south of Breda, and they had dined and danced and talked —not serious talk, Leo wasn't any good at that, his conversation was gay and witty and amusing and sometimes malicious, but Gemma hardly noticed

84

that. She basked in his admiration and felt for the first time in her life that perhaps she wasn't quite as plain as she had supposed herself to be.

It never occurred to her that he found her amusingly unsophisticated, even at times a little dull; it certainly didn't occur to her that he didn't mean a word he said. She only knew that she had met someone who treated her like a queen, had even become, miraculously, attracted to her, and because she was honest herself she made no secret of her interest in him. All the same, she tried not to let him see it too much—indeed, when he reached out to take hold of her hand across the table, she withdrew it in a matter-of-fact way which nonplussed him for the minute. He changed his tactics then, telling her about Holland, making her laugh at the odd tales and legends he told with such ease, and he didn't touch her again, not even when he drew up outside the door of Huis Berhuys and leant across to open the door for her. He didn't get out, though, but wished her an airy goodnight and without another word about seeing her again, drove away. Gemma watched him go and shivered a little; perhaps she had imagined that he liked her ... she got the key from her purse and was about to open the door when it was opened for her. The professor ushered her in, looking absent-minded. He waved the book he held at her and murmured: 'I was reading and heard the car. Didn't Leo want to come in?'

She lifted a rather unhappy face to his. 'I don't know—I didn't ask him. I think he was in a hurry to get home.'

Her companion nodded. 'Probably. I hope you had a pleasant evening? Where did you go?'

She told him, still feeling not quite happy; she had been deposited at the door in a rather summary fashion, surely? Mandy and Phil, when they went out in the evening, were always ushered carefully in through their front door by their companions. Perhaps the Dutch had different views about such things. She frowned a little and the professor said comfortably: 'Rienieta is sleeping soundly—so is everyone else. Come and share my coffee before you go to bed and you can tell me all about your evening.' He smiled at her. 'I'm not *au fait* with gay nights.'

Gemma preceded him across the hall and into the pleasant cosiness of the library. 'Well, you ought to be,' she said a trifle tartly. 'There's no reason why you shouldn't be; you can take your pick of pretty girls and go where you like . . .'

'Most girls look exactly alike to me,' he confessed mildly, and pushed her gently into a chair. 'Be mother and pour the coffee. Perhaps I'm getting too old.'

'Don't talk rubbish,' she begged him. 'You're not in the least old.'

'Thank you, Gemma.' He settled his length in a chair close to hers. 'I like four lumps, please.'

She handed him his cup and because the silence seemed a little long, asked: 'Are you staying the night?'

'Yes. I—er—missed an engagement this evening and it seemed more sensible to go back to Vianen in the morning.' He leaned back, very much at his ease. 'Did you dance?'

'Oh, yes—Leo dances very well, you know, though I'm not so keen on this modern style.'

'Ah—he'll be taking you again, I dare say.'

She gave him a rather bleak look. 'I don't know, he didn't say.'

The professor's eyes narrowed. 'He will.' He became all at once brisk. 'Finished your coffee? Off to bed with you, then, and leave me in peace to finish this most interesting book.' He got to his feet, his smile robbing the words of abruptness. 'Dream of your splendid evening, Gemma. Goodnight.'

CHAPTER FIVE

GEMMA hadn't expected to see the professor the next morning, but when she went along to Rienieta's room there he was, sitting on the window seat with his feet up, listening with every sign of close interest to whatever it was that his sister was talking about so earnestly. She was speaking Dutch, but when she saw Gemma she switched at once to English. 'Hullo, Gemma, I'm telling Ross that I'm quite well again . . .'

Gemma made some casual reply and wished the professor good morning, suppressing the strong suspicion that Rienieta hadn't been talking about herself at all, but her nurse. The professor had got to his feet, given his sister a brotherly hug, nodded cheerfully to Gemma and wandered away.

The door had barely closed behind him when Rienieta burst out: 'Well, did you have a lovely evening? Where did you go? What did you do? Did Leo admire your dress?'

'He didn't say,' said Gemma lightly.

'How horrid of him, for you looked very pretty. I should have been angry with him.' She tossed her pretty head and then smiled with great charm. 'Shall I tell you a secret?'

She was like a pretty child with her beguiling

ways. Gemma found herself returning the smile. 'Well, no, love—if it's a secret, it won't be any longer if you tell it.'

The invalid frowned over this and then her brow cleared. 'It's not that kind of secret. Ross came to take you out yesterday, only he didn't know about Leo calling for you—imagine, two dates in one evening!' She giggled. 'You must be very sexy, Gemma.'

Gemma said a little absently that no, she didn't think she was, while she digested the news that the professor had come to take her out, and while she didn't feel the same excitement that she had felt at Leo's invitation, there was a pleasant glow inside her at the thought of it, dispelled at once by Rienieta saying airily: 'I expect he thought he'd better keep you sweet—you haven't had much time to yourself, have you? and you hadn't been out at all. Perhaps he was afraid that you would be tired of the job.'

Perhaps he was. Gemma shook pills from a bottle. 'No,' she said quietly, 'I'm not tired of the job, and I certainly don't expect to be taken out just to keep me sweet.'

'The trouble with you is that you're too nice,' declared her companion. 'If I were you, I would want to be amused after spending hours with me. Am I very tiresome?'

The blue eyes were anxious. 'Oh, lord, no,' laughed Gemma, 'you're not tiresome at all—why should you think that? And I'm not at all overworked, you know—I feel as though I'm on holiday.'

'Even when I ring the bell in the middle of the night just because I am fed up?'

'Even then, and that doesn't happen often, does it? You'll be as good as new in another week or two.'

'That's what Ross said, and he never tells fibs.' Rienieta asked after a pause: 'Do you like him?'

'Yes.' Gemma meant that; she did like him; he had a nice habit of turning up at the right moment. 'What would you like for your breakfast?' she asked briskly.

The professor had gone by the time she went downstairs. She would have liked to have spent an hour or two in his company, telling him about Leo and the lovely time she had had and how wonderful she had felt and how doubtful she felt now—a rather ridiculous wish, really, but that hadn't occurred to her; all she knew was that she could tell him things she wouldn't dream of telling anyone else.

There wasn't anyone at the breakfast table by the time she got there, either. Old Doctor Dieperink van Berhuys had gone to Breda where he still had a small consulting practice with two partners, and his wife had gone with him. Gemma exchanged good mornings with Ignaas who had brought in fresh coffee for her and sat down to her lonely meal.

But at least there were letters for her; a thick envelope with news from each of her brothers and sisters as well as a long, neatly written one from Cousin Maud, in which she was told to have a good time while she was in Holland. 'And,' Maud suggested, 'if you want to, when your job is finished, why don't you go to Amsterdam and have a look round? I'm sure Ross would know of some inexpensive, quiet hotel.'

Gemma smiled as she read this; Ross, she felt sure, if he felt the need to stay in a hotel in Amsterdam, would go to the Amstel or the Doelen; she doubted very much if he had ever poked his high-bridged nose into any lesser establishment. She put down Maud's letter and picked up the last envelope. From Matron, bless her, hoping that she was happy and implying, in the nicest possible way, that there would be no job for her when she got back; there was some dispute about the number of geriatric beds and the fire had given some of the more cheese-paring members of the board to press for a cut in the number of patients as well as nurses. Matron expressed the hope that Gemma might find herself a nice, well-paid job in Holland; probably she would have the opportunity of looking around for herself and inquiring at some of the larger hospitals. Utrecht or Leiden, wrote Matron knowledgeably, were renowned for their teaching hospitals and Gemma was sufficiently highly qualified to apply for any post she chose.

Gemma folded the letter thoughtfully. She saw very little chance of going to either Utrecht or Leiden and still less of seeing the inside of any hospital; she would have to look around the moment she got back to England—London was a safe bet, of course; her own training hospital would give her a job if there was one going, but then she wouldn't be home each day to help Cousin Maud. She would have to think about it.

She was about to leave the table when Ria came to tell her that she was wanted on the telephone. She tried not to hurry across the hall; it was absurd how breathless she felt at the prospect of hearing Leo's voice again. Only it wasn't Leo, it was Bart, wanting to know if she would like to go to the Annual Ball at his hospital. 'Saturday,' he told her, 'so you have two days to arrange things, and that shouldn't be difficult because Iny will be home for days off and she'll keep an eye on Rienieta. And you are to wear the pink dress you wore the other evening.'

Gemma didn't remember that he had seen her in it, but probably Rienieta had told him about it. Her head was so nicely full of excited thoughts that she quite forgot about Leo; did he think, she asked anxiously, that two evenings out in one week seemed rather a lot? She listened to his reassurances, admitted that she hadn't had much free time so far, and promised she would ask if anyone would mind.

They didn't; she was urged to accept, plans were made for Doctor Dieperink van Berhuys to drive her to Utrecht where Bart would meet her, and so much interest was displayed in what she intended to wear and how she would do her hair that she was made to feel quite important. She forbore to mention that she had only the pink dress, anyway—and as for her hair, she decided to do it as she always did, otherwise it might come adrift and spoil her evening.

Rienieta was improving steadily now; there had been almost no fever for two days, although she still had aching joints if she attempted to do too much. Gemma let her do a little more each day, playing with the puppies, playing endless games of cards, discussing clothes, and never lacking something to talk about. They got on well together, and Rienieta regaled her with tales of her family, only she never seemed to have much to say about Ross. It was surprising, mused Gemma, that he seemed such a casual yet candid person, and yet the very whereabouts of his home was a secret to her. She brushed his image aside and concentrated upon Leo, but he hadn't taken any notice of her since they had had their evening together, so she brushed him aside too, which wasn't so easy.

She spent the whole of Saturday in a state of apprehension, afraid that Rienieta would develop a temperature and have another relapse so that she would be unable to go to the ball, but she remained in quite excellent health, and Gemma, having dealt with pills, instructions for going to bed and any emergency which could possibly arise, retired to her room to dress, to reappear just as Ignaas was coming up the stairs to tell her that Doctor Dieperink van Berhuys was ready to leave. She flew to say goodnight to Rienieta and Iny and skipped downstairs, where she found Rienieta's mother waiting to wish her a pleasant evening and offer, in the most tactful way, a soft white shawl.

'Too warm for a coat,' she observed tactfully, 'but you might need a wrap when you return.' Her nice little face broke into a smile. 'Don't let Bart drive too fast, my dear.' Bart was to bring Gemma back and stay the night.

Ross's father had very much the same manner as his eldest son; he was almost as placid and he drove just as fast. Gemma hardly noticed the journey; she

93

chatted away happily, led on by his quiet questions and comments, laughing at his small jokes, so that by the time they arrived at the hospital she was in exactly the right mood for a super evening. She thanked him prettily for bringing her, expressed the hope that he would drive carefully home again, and allowed herself to be handed over to Bart, who said at once to win her heart: 'Ah, the pink dress—good!'

She went at once to tidy her hair and dispose of the shawl and went back to the entrance hall to join him again. There were a great many people there and from what she could see of the women around her, her dress was barely adequate—still, as long as Bart found it pretty ... They took to the dance floor and Gemma forgot everything else but the pleasure of dancing. They had circled the floor perhaps twice when Leo took Bart's place with a careless: 'Thanks, old chap,' and a smile for her which set her heart beating nineteen to the dozen. 'Surprised?' he wanted to know. 'I got Bart to fix it ...'

'Why?'

He looked taken aback. 'Well, I thought it would be fun—besides, I thought that the van Berhuys might object.'

'Object?' She was quite bewildered. 'Why should they? You're a friend of the family.'

'Oh, rather—known them for years.' He smiled his charming smile again. 'I wanted to keep it a secret—you and me. People don't believe in love at first sight any more.'

'Don't they?' Her heart was dancing a jig. 'I can't

94

think why not; there must be dozens of ways of falling in love, so why not at first sight?'

'A sensible darling, aren't you? We're going to have a lovely evening together and I shall drive you home afterwards.'

She looked at him with delight, then said regretfully: 'I can't come with you, Leo. I promised his mother that I would see that Bart didn't drive too fast.'

Leo looked annoyed, but she didn't see that, only heard him say carelessly: 'Oh, well, we'll sort that out later, shall we?'

The music had stopped, but he didn't let her go. 'Come and meet some of my friends,' he invited, and caught her hand in his. There was no sign of Bart and the place was packed now; it would be hopeless to look for him, so Gemma allowed herself to be led across the room to a rather noisy group, the young men long-haired and extravagantly dressed, the girls in dresses which Gemma thought privately weren't quite decent even if they had cost a fortune. She smiled and murmured her way around the circle and everyone asked her a great many questions in too loud voices while they eyed her dress with thinly veiled amusement. Gemma saw the look and her small chin lifted, but the situation was saved by one of the young men, who swept her off to dance so that the unpleasant moment passed. He danced well but a little wildly, singing in her ear and holding her so tightly that she could hardly breathe. She resigned herself to ten minutes or so of his company before, surely, Leo would rescue her.

It wasn't Leo who rescued her. They had reached the comparatively empty space at the bottom of the ballroom when her companion said, far too loudly: 'This is the stuffed shirt end—the professors and deans and clever dicks ...'

Ross was there, sitting at one of the small tables with another older man and two rather matronly women with nice faces, and although she hadn't meant to, Gemma gave him an appealing glance as they passed the table and whirled away again. He was the last person she had expected to see there, and probably he was just as surprised to see her ... Her partner disappeared and the professor was in his place, dancing her quite beautifully down the ballroom.

'Hullo,' he said matter-of-factly. 'I hope I interpreted that look correctly. It was rescue you wanted, wasn't it?'

'Oh, yes, thank you,' said Gemma fervently, aware that he danced a good deal better than Bart or Leo and certainly far better than the noisy type she had just endured. 'I'm not sure who he was—a friend of Leo's ...' She paused and the professor said noncommittally:

'Ah, yes—I saw him. Where is Bart?'

'Bart? Well—I haven't seen him just lately ...' She didn't see the rather grim expression on her companion's face. 'He's taking me home,' she added, aware somehow that the professor needed placating and not sure why. She added, because he was a man one didn't try to sidetrack: 'Leo said he would, but I said no because your mother asked me most particularly to see that Bart didn't drive too fast.'

'Ah, yes,' murmured her partner, which told her nothing at all and was the kind of annoying answer to dry up any conversation. 'Come and meet a few friends of mine,' he invited, and she found herself sitting at the little table, drinking something or other, drawn into the friendly talk of the older man, who was the dean, and the two women, one of whom was his wife. Presently another man came over to join them and the dean, making little jokes about his age, asked Gemma to dance. They circled the room sedately and she saw that the professor was dancing with the dean's wife, although she couldn't see Bart anywhere, or Leo—but somehow she didn't mind very much; this was better than having to talk to Leo's friends, even though it wasn't very exciting.

The dance ended and they went back to their table. Gemma finished her drink and hoped that the professor would ask her to dance again, but he showed no inclination to do so, and when Bart suddenly appeared and invited her to take the floor with him, she did so, wondering what it was that the professor had uttered low-voiced to his brother to make him look so defiant and sulky. She set herself to cheer him up, but her good intentions were cut short by the reappearance of Leo, who slid smoothly into Bart's place and danced her off the floor and into one of the small rooms leading out of the ballroom.

'Lord, what a crush!' he complained. 'I saw you entangled with the elderlies and sent Bart along to rescue you.' He was holding her hand, but she withdrew it gently.

'I didn't find them elderly,' she told him, 'and why didn't you do the rescuing yourself?'

He grinned like a small boy and Gemma found herself smiling back at him. 'You must have guessed by now that Ross doesn't like me overmuch—we keep out of each other's way and we're civil when we meet, of course, but he's a good deal older than I am, isn't he, and we have very little in common. Being so learned makes him a bit of a bore and rather a dull fellow.' He had taken her hand again and she let it lie.

'You're wrong, of course,' she told him quietly. 'He's not dull and he's certainly not a bore ...'

'My darling girl, he shall be none of these things if you say so—now let's talk about us.' He pulled her to him and kissed her, and Gemma, who had been hoping that he would do just that, was disappointed to find that it wasn't what she had expected—oh, it was thrilling all right, but something was lacking. Perhaps she was too excited to enjoy it. She kissed him back a little awkwardly and said shyly: 'I can't think what you can see in me.'

His answer was more than satisfactory, but then it should have been, for had she but known it he had had considerable practice in such matters with other girls. But she didn't know it, so she took his words at their face value, cherishing every one of them to remember later.

They danced again presently, and Gemma, caught up in daydreams and excitement and the heady belief that Leo thought her a wonderful girl, looked for once almost pretty, so that the professor, treading a sober foxtrot with the dean's wife again, looked at her thoughtfully and while carrying on a desultory conversation with his partner, allowed his powerful brain to assess the situation. But none of this showed on his calm features. He bent his head to listen to some triviality uttered by his partner, and when he caught Gemma's eye as she flashed past them in a more up-to-date version of the dance, his faint smile betokened polite recognition and nothing more.

The end of the evening came too soon for Gemma; she had danced almost every dance with Leo, although between them she had had to endure the brittle friendliness of his companions, but that had been a small price to pay for the delight of his company. As for the professor, she had glimpsed him from time to time, and presently forgot him completely.

Leo had said nothing more about taking her home, and although she would have liked to have gone with him more than anything else, she had put it out of her mind, and supposed that he had done the same. She fetched the shawl from the mass of evening wraps and fur coats and repaired to the entrance hall to wait for Bart, but the minutes passed and the crowds thinned rapidly; she was beginning to feel anxious when Leo joined her.

'Sorry you were left alone,' he said solicitously, 'but Bart isn't feeling well—had too much to drink, I shouldn't wonder, so it looks as though I'm going to get my wish after all; someone has to take you home and there's nothing I'd like more.'

Gemma hesitated. 'Ought I to see Bart first?' she asked. 'His mother might want to know why he didn't come home—I'm not sure ...'

'I've messages from him—you weren't to worry, for a start, and will you make it all right with his mother, and he'll telephone in the morning.'

It didn't sound quite like Bart. 'Oh, well, all right,' she said at length. She was still hesitating and Leo frowned a little.

'You don't seem very pleased at the prospect of my company.'

He sounded cool and she hastened to say: 'Oh, but I am, really I am, only I'm sorry about Bart.'

'He's in good hands; he'll be as right as rain in no time—he's had the sense to know that he's in no fit state to drive.' He tucked a hand under her arm. 'Let's go, shall we?'

She accompanied him happily enough to the entrance; it was hard luck on Bart, but as things turned out, convenient for her. She went through the big double doors of the hospital and walked into the professor's large and solid back.

It wasn't Leo's hand on her arm any more, but the professor's, and Leo was standing a little apart, looking sulky.

'You took a long time,' observed the professor, and although his voice was mild it held a silkiness which gave Gemma the nasty feeling that he was in a riproaring temper, but she had no need to reply, for he went on in Dutch, addressing himself to Leo. Leo answered him presently, sounding as sulky as he looked, and Gemma looking from one to other of them in bewilderment, was relieved when the professor said in English:

'A little misunderstanding—Bart isn't fit to drive, but as I'm going home anyway, I'll take you with me.' He glanced at Leo. 'Good of you to offer Gemma a lift,' he remarked in a voice which suggested that there was nothing good about it. 'Goodnight.'

He didn't give Gemma a chance to say more than goodnight herself, but swung her round and marched her across the courtyard to where a white Jaguar XL-S was parked. The professor opened its door and ushered her in smartly and she said crossly: 'This isn't your car,' her world so awry for the moment that she would have liked to have burst into tears or given him a good thump, only with the size of him, she wouldn't have done much damage.

'Er—yes, it is. Now don't be a silly girl—get in.'

Gemma snorted. Now she was a silly girl, was she, to be ordered about and have her evening ruined, and bullied into the bargain! She got into the luxurious seat with dignity without looking at him and then forgot all about being dignified, for Bart was sitting in the back. It was a handsome car, meant for two but with space for an occasional third, and he looked a little cramped. He said hullo in a sheepish voice, and startled out of her own not very happy thoughts, she exclaimed: 'Bart—Leo said you weren't feeling quite the thing ...' She looked at him anxiously, for he was a nice boy; the twins would be like him in a year or two ... 'Shouldn't you be in bed?'

'He will be in bed soon enough,' observed the professor, easing himself into the seat beside her, 'and he can start sleeping it off now—it's only a hangover, but my dear Bart, if you will drink vodka in such quantities, that is to be expected.'

'It was a joke.' Bart still sounded sheepish.

'I know that, but a thoughtless one. It was known that you were to drive Gemma back, was it not?'

'Yes, of course. I told Leo—probably he forgot.'

'Probably he did,' said his brother in a dry voice.

Gemma was only half listening. As the big car slid out of the hospital courtyard and into the city streets, she muttered in a voice she strove to keep even, 'I can't quite see why you should have to take me home, Professor.'

He glanced at her briefly. 'Spoilt your evening, have I? Don't worry, Gemma, Leo always gets what he sets his heart on—that is, almost always.'

'That's hardly the point, is it? You just—just ...'

'Gummed up the works? Yes, I did.' He added impatiently: 'Why do you have to be such a child—the eldest of six and still wet behind the ears!'

This inelegant speech had the effect of rendering her speechless for several seconds until she managed in a furious voice: 'You're rude and arrogant and —and you're a bully too ...'

'Anything you say,' he agreed blandly, and she reflected uneasily that although he had spoken so quietly he was probably holding a very nasty temper in check. The perverse urge to annoy him still more

102

took hold of her, so that she went on recklessly: 'I was having a simply lovely time and I'm perfectly able to look after myself—Leo would have taken me home.' She added nastily: 'And I should have enjoyed that.'

The professor laughed. 'Vixen!' he murmured. 'I'm sorry you're so upset, but it will do no harm, you know—Leo enjoys a good chase and I promise you that I won't be there to spoil things next time. Am I forgiven?'

Gemma had never quarrelled for more than half an hour with anyone and she never bore a grudge. She said willingly enough, 'Yes, all right, but I don't want to talk about it any more.'

They were on the motorway and the Jaguar was making light of the kilometres. Just as though they hadn't had a single cross word, the professor remarked easily: 'You met a great many people this evening. How did you like the dean and his wife?'

'Nice,' pronounced Gemma. 'He's a poppet, and she was so kind—in the same way as your mother is kind. One can talk to people like that and they listen in a cosy way, but they're never inquisitive.'

He nodded. 'And what about the crowd Leo runs with?'

She stirred uneasily. 'Well, I'm not used to people like that—clever and smart and one never quite knows if they're serious or not—can you imagine them in the village at home? You see, I'm not clever or witty and I can't talk like they do—I felt an ig-ig . . .'

'Ignoramus,' he supplied gravely. 'But not really;

they would feel the same if someone put them into the middle of a hospital ward and told them to take the temperatures. They're in their element at a night club, and you're in yours flinging old ladies down fire chutes and making tea at one o'clock in the morning without so much as a frown.' They were approaching Rosendaal and he slowed a little. 'Talking of tea, I think we shall have to revive Bart with some black coffee when we get in.'

'He'll be all right in the morning?'

'He'd better be; I've no intention of Mama finding out that he was pickled in vodka.'

It gave her a pleasant feeling, knowing that the professor stood by his brothers and sisters when they needed it after some petty misdemeanour. She said suddenly: 'I'm sorry I said all that about you just now. None of it was true—it's jolly decent of you to cover up for Bart.'

He thanked her blandly. 'But you would do the same?'

'Of course—the eldest always does.' She frowned into the motorway ahead, clearly seen in the car's headlights. 'You said pickled with vodka.'

'Just that. He was dared to drink a glass of the stuff, and he did, silly chap, between Pilseners, and then, for a joke it seems, someone laced his next few Pilseners with more of the stuff. He was out cold when I found him.'

'Found him? Did they leave him like that?'

'Yes.'

'It must have been one of those friends of Leo's —they were rather wild.'

'Probably.' Gemma waited for him to continue, but he didn't, so she went on: 'Leo said Bart had a bit of a headache and was a bit under the weather; if he'd known, he would have done something about it.'

'Oh, undoubtedly,' agreed the professor gently.

'Have you known him long?' Her head was full of Leo again.

'De Vos? All our lives—he is ten years younger than I.'

'He's great fun.' Her voice was a little high in her efforts to keep it casual.

'Indeed yes. I gather that you—er—like him.'

'I do.' She was in full spate now, longing to tell someone how she felt about Leo, and this placid man beside her, despite his unexpected, quickly damped down anger, seemed to fulfil the role of confidant to the manner born. 'You see, no one has ever treated me like that before—looked at me as though I was pretty, and told me I was even though I know I'm not, and—and telephoned me ... and I never knew that he would be at the ball—it was a super surprise. I wish I had another dress, though, this one wasn't nearly grand enough.'

The professor made a small sound. He said in a kind voice: 'I thought it was charming, and so did the dean.'

She thanked him; it was the kind of remark she might have expected from him, although she could hardly say that the dean's opinion of her dress didn't matter a fig to her; it was Leo she wanted to please.

There was a companionable silence between them

until she asked: 'Do you really suppose he'll ask me out again?'

'Of course he will. I should buy a new dress, if I were you—it won't be wasted.'

They were almost home. Gemma turned to look at Bart, snoring behind them; at least she would be able to say with perfect truth that he hadn't driven fast. As though he had read her thoughts, the professor said:

'I'll tell Mama that I decided to come home and drive you both—there's no need to say more than that.'

'Very well.' He turned the car in at the gates and stopped in front of the door; there was a faint light showing through the transom above it but the rest of the house was in darkness. He got out and opened the door, then came back for her, and when she was safely inside he went back to rouse Bart.

'Coffee in the kitchen?' inquired Gemma. She spoke in a whisper, because the dim quiet of the hall made it impossible to do otherwise.

The professor nodded, his arm round Bart, who, half awake, was complaining about his head. 'Oh, do hush him,' she said urgently, and led the way across the hall.

There was coffee on the Aga; it took only a moment to find three mugs and the sugar, sit Bart down in a chair and urge him to drink up. He did it reluctantly at first, but by the time he had downed the second cup he was feeling decidedly better. 'So sorry,' he said apologetically, 'made an ass of myself.'

'No, you didn't,' said Gemma in a comforting

voice. 'You weren't to know about the rest of that vodka—it was a rotten trick to play on you. Do you begin to feel better?'

She filled his cup for the third time and offered the silent professor another mugful. 'Yes, thanks, Gemma—you're a good sort not to mind.'

He sounded like one of her twin brothers and she gave him a motherly smile and got to her feet. 'I'll get these out of the way and go to bed.'

She tidied away neatly, thanked Bart for her lovely evening with a sincerity which allowed of no sarcasm and started for the door, to find the professor beside her long before she reached it. She said goodnight as he opened it, but he followed her into the hall and she asked: 'Is something the matter? Did you want to say something about Bart?'

'Not about Bart—about you, Gemma. You have had your happy evening spoilt and you've been a darling about it. You're a gem of a girl, do you know that? I hope all your dreams come true, for you deserve them.'

Before she could reply he bent to kiss her—not at all the same kind of kiss which Leo had given her, for it was gentle and brief. She knew that long after the heady excitement of Leo's kiss had faded, she would remember this moment. She said 'Oh,' rather blankly and ran up the staircase without looking back.

CHAPTER SIX

To her surprise, Gemma slept at once and dreamlessly, to wake at her usual time feeling quite refreshed. Rienieta was already awake when she went along to see how she was, and they whiled away half an hour talking about the ball, Gemma doing her best to answer her companion's eager questions. Fortunately she had a good memory; she was able to give detailed descriptions of a number of the dresses there, the food she had eaten and the people she had met, and even a few of their names.

'And Bart?' asked Rienieta. 'Was he waiting for you? Papa said you looked so pretty that he would have liked to stay and dance with you—he joked, of course,' she added seriously. 'He would never go anywhere without Mama.'

'No, of course he wouldn't,' Gemma agreed, 'but how nice of him to say that.' She launched into an account of Bart's prowess as a dancer, and mentioned casually that Leo had been there too.

Her patient was examining her tongue in a hand mirror. She put it back in to say: 'I—We are not surprised. Mama said yesterday that she was afraid that he would be there too—he and his friends. Were they there, Gemma?'

Gemma charted her patient's temperature with a

steady hand. 'Oh, yes—rather silly I thought, not quite my cup of tea. The girls wore those lovely impossible dresses you see in *Vogue*.' She smiled at Rienieta as she shook down the thermometer. 'Your mother doesn't like Leo?'

'She understands that he is great fun ...'

'But she would prefer me not to go out with him. Well, I can understand that—we haven't the same background. I'm middle class, you know, and neither clever nor smart.' She hesitated. 'I hadn't thought of it before, but I can see now that if I had someone like me working for me, I wouldn't want me to go tearing off with the upper crust.'

Rienieta's blue eyes grew round, but it was the professor's voice that answered her. He was standing in the doorway watching her and smiling a little. 'What a very muddled way of putting it, Gemma, but you don't do yourself justice; such an idea would never enter Mama's head and certainly not my father's—nor anyone else in the family, for that matter. It's no use telling you that you are far too good for de Vos; but if he has been lucky enough to win your regard then none of us, I can promise you, will lift a finger to prevent you seeing him as often as it can be arranged.'

Gemma's eyes were as round as her patient's, her face remarkably flushed. She tried to think of something to say and found that her usually sensible head was quite empty, but as it turned out there was no need to say anything at all, for he came wandering into the room, saying easily: 'I thought you might like to know that Bart is more or less himself—he looks washed out, but that can be put down to too much dancing. Are you coming down to breakfast?'

'No—yes,' said Gemma wildly. 'I hadn't thought about it—I must see to Rienieta . . .'

'I see no reason why she shouldn't, just this once, come down too. It will—er—distract attention . . .'

'Why?' asked his sister. 'What's Bart been doing? Tell, or I won't help.'

'He's done nothing, brat; he was a bit under the weather last night, so I brought him back with Gemma and stayed the night.'

'Drunk?' inquired Rienieta wisely.

'A nasty word,' reproved her brother. 'Bart doesn't get drunk—he drank something by mistake, though, and it made him feel wretched. Mama is not to know.'

'O.K. Though I don't mind betting you that she'll find out. She always does, you know—you always find things out, too, don't you, Ross? Only you never tell anyone . . .'

'A gift.' His voice was amiable. 'Don't you wish you had it? Now, how about breakfast?'

The meal was noisy and talkative because so many members of the family were there and Rienieta, undoubtedly the family darling, was in tearing spirits. Probably we shall have tears by teatime, thought Gemma gloomily, watching her. All the same, she was almost recovered from her illness and she had had no fever for several days. Soon she would be pronounced well and she herself would go back to England. She didn't want to go, and not only because of Leo; she liked Holland and she liked the people

110

with whom she was sharing her breakfast; she would miss them dreadfully. She looked round the table and caught the professor's eye, and when he smiled her vague worries about leaving disappeared.

He and Bart went shortly afterwards, and Gemma, busy with her patient, had no chance to say goodbye, although she heard the car leave. The house seemed very quiet for the rest of the day and it wasn't until the end of the day, while she was helping Rienieta to bed, that Leo telephoned. His voice sounded gay in her ear as well as tender, and to begin with, apologetic.

'About last night,' he began, 'sorry about the mix-up; there wasn't much I could do, though, and I knew you'd get home safely enough with Ross.' He laughed softly as though he found that funny. 'But, lord, I was disappointed, I can tell you. You're not in disgrace or anything like that, sweetheart?'

'Disgrace? Why ever should I be?' asked Gemma, savouring the sweetheart part.

'Oh, nothing. Have you used up all your free time, or could we have a quick run this evening?'

'Not this evening.' She hoped her voice sounded firm; she would have loved to have said yes, but she had come as Rienieta's nurse and even though there wasn't much for her to do, she was still employed as such.

'Tomorrow, then?'

'Well, that would be nice, but I must ask first, and then only for an hour or so after Rienieta is in bed.'

'Splendid. I'll be outside about half past eight. They dine at seven, don't they?'

'Yes. Goodbye, Leo.'

She wore a jersey dress this time and took a cardigan and scarf with her because Rienieta had warned her that Leo drove an open sports car as well as the BMW he had taken her out in before. She was glad of the advice when she saw that the car was a Porsche—a 911S Targa. Leo didn't get out when he saw her, but leaned across to open the door, said briefly: 'Hop in, darling,' and sped out into the road almost before Gemma had settled herself.

'How about den Haag?' he inquired.

She knotted the scarf firmly under her chin before replying. 'That's too far, Leo—I said an hour.'

He looked annoyed. 'Good lord, I didn't think you meant that—why, an hour is just a waste of an evening.'

'In that case, stop, turn round and take me back again,' she said crisply.

Her words had the effect of making him laugh. 'I've never met anyone quite like you,' he told her, 'but all right, little darling, an hour it shall be.'

He was driving fast and rather recklessly. 'We'll go to my place and have a drink and I promise you I'll take you back in an hour's time.'

'Where is your place?'

'Just off the motorway, going towards Breda—quite close by. I've a few friends staying with me—I think you met some of them last night ... and what a dreary affair that was!'

'I enjoyed it very much.' Gemma frowned a little, for they seemed at outs with one another. 'But then I don't go out a great deal; there's nothing much in the village where I live; a few dinner parties and tennis in the summer—anyway, I haven't much time ...'

'My poor darling, it must be utterly ghastly looking after the sick—and you don't have to pretend that you like it to me.'

'But I do like it. Leo, what happened to Bart yesterday evening?'

He had turned into a narrow country road and was hooting impatiently because there was a cattle lorry ahead of him. 'Bart? Oh, the young idiot drank some vodka and passed out—I didn't tell you because I didn't want to upset you.' He smiled at her and she glowed under it.

'You look lovely,' he uttered the trite words with practised charm and then turned away to curse the lorry driver in Dutch as he skidded past him. 'Shouldn't allow the fellows on the roads,' he grumbled, and then: 'Here we are.'

The house stood back from the road, smaller than Huis Berhuys and built of brick in a rather pretentious style. Gemma didn't like it much, although she was prepared to try because it was Leo's home. The evening was warm, the windows were open, showing a brightly lighted interior and allowing a good deal of noise to escape; his few friends must be enjoying themselves, Gemma decided as she got out of the car and, obedient to his nod, walked into the hall, a dark apartment with a good deal of carved furniture in it and painted leather walls. The sitting room, in contrast, was brilliantly lighted and full of people, she saw that at once as Leo drew her into it with a hand on her arm, and she had met several of them, just as he had said. She realized a little late in the day that she was too tired to join in the bright froth of chatter going on around her and which seemed to be their sole conversation, but she smiled and nodded and said hullo and accepted the glass Leo gave her—champagne. She took a sip and wrinkled her nose at its dryness, and Leo, a careless arm flung around her shoulders, asked laughingly: 'Never had it before, Gemma?'

Everyone laughed when she said seriously: 'Not often, birthday parties and things like that,' and the harmless remark sparked up a great many witty remarks about nothing much so that she allowed her gaze to wander round the room. It was furnished in a heavy style she didn't much care for, although there were some pictures on its walls she would have liked to have examined, but her eye lighted on the gilt clock above the marble chimneypiece and she said at once: 'Leo, I should like to go back, please—we've been gone an hour already.'

'Of course, darling. Just one more glass of champagne first—Cor, go out and turn the car for me, will you?' He turned back to Gemma. 'Darling, we've hardly spoken to each other, we'll have to do better than this.'

She wished silently that he wouldn't call her darling so often, it made the word meaningless. 'I'm going back to England soon,' she told him.

'Then we must arrange something ...' His smile came and went. 'England's not so far away, you know.' He went on in a concerned way: 'You're

114

getting worried about getting back, aren't you? We'll go this very moment.'

She smiled her gratitude. 'I'm sorry, it was hardly worth you coming to take me out, was it?'

He said in her ear: 'Even five minutes of your company would be worth a whole evening's travel.' She didn't quite believe that, but it was a nice thing to have said of one. They left the house on a noisy wave of goodbyes and laughter. Leo's friends laughed a good deal about nothing much.

Leo drove straight back to Huis Berhuys; he drove fast but much more carefully this time, and when they got there he got out and opened the car door for Gemma and walked with her to where Ignaas was waiting at the house door. He waited until the door had been closed behind her after wishing her a restrained goodbye under the old man's eye—a goodbye hinting at hidden devotion and suppressed eagerness—and then got back into his car and drove away, very well pleased with himself. It had taken him a little while to discover that Gemma was distinctly old-fashioned; he was going to get nowhere with her with champagne and parties. She might be unsophisticated, but she wasn't a fool either. He grinned to himself; his technique with girls had never failed, and it wasn't going to now, only he would have to work fast if she was going back to England so soon. He began planning the next outing—lunch at a rather staid restaurant perhaps, it might be a bit boring. He would have to tell Cor and the others ... He drove on, his mind nicely occupied.

Gemma, happily unaware of Leo's plans, thanked Ignaas for opening the door, remarked, in the handful of Dutch words she had acquired, that it was a nice evening and went upstairs to find Rienieta sitting up in bed with the telephone clamped to her ear.

She waved as Gemma went in, said something into the receiver and then: 'It's Ross, he wants to speak to you.'

Gemma came down from the romantic cloud she had been floating upon and took the receiver, sat down on the side of the bed and said briskly: 'Hullo, Professor.'

'Gemma? I want you to bring Rienieta to Utrecht tomorrow—she's to have a complete check-up, it's something we feel should be done; she seems cured and probably is, but as you know it's an illness which is sometimes more serious in an adult. She can stay overnight in the hospital and you will stay with her, if you will, although you won't be needed a great deal.' His voice, impersonal until now, became warm and friendly. 'It will give you a chance to see something of Utrecht.'

Gemma, her feet firmly on the ground again, said yes, how nice and at what time were they to be ready?

'I'm coming down in the morning—if I can manage to get away I shall come this evening, but I don't know yet, and I'll take you both back with me after breakfast. Father has to come up to Utrecht and he will drive you both home again.' There was a little silence. 'You haven't made any arrangements for yourself?'

'None.' Gemma was still brisk, nudging aside the thought that probably Leo would have telephoned later and made another date. Oh, well, absence made the heart grow fonder, didn't it? And what was two days? Anyway, they might be back in time for her to spend an evening with him. She said good-bye and handed the receiver back to Rienieta, who embarked on a long conversation in her own language. When she finally put the telephone down she said at once: 'I say, won't it be super? I hate hospitals, but if Ross is there and you are too—you don't mind coming? I don't suppose there'll be anything to do but just to have you with me ... you're so reassuring, Gemma.'

The big blue eyes filled with tears and Gemma hurried over to the bed and put her arms round her patient's shoulders. 'Now, now, love, there's nothing to be scared about—it's just a routine check-up. I don't suppose it will take more than an hour or two and I won't be far away, I promise you.'

'You really promise?'

'Promise—cross my heart and hope to die.' She produced a clean handkerchief and handed it to the still sniffing Rienieta. 'Now, what will you wear?'

Her patient brightened. 'I've a new dress ...'

'Splendid, just as long as it's easy to get out of and into. Remember you will be tired after the journey and for certain they'll want you to go to bed at once so that you're nicely rested ready for the tests and so on.'

'It's a denim pinafore with a white blouse—it has

a drawstring neck and long sleeves with lots of buttons at the wrist, only there is no need to undo them.'

'Sounds ideal, but supposing we ask your mother what she thinks?' Gemma went to the door. 'Will she be in the drawing room?'

'Yes, it isn't eleven o'clock yet and she never goes to bed until then.'

'Then I'll ask her to come up again even though she's been up to say goodnight to you, but if I fetch her will you promise to go straight to sleep afterwards?'

'Cross my heart,' said Rienieta seriously.

Her mother was sitting in the small armchair she always used, knitting. She was wearing glasses a little crooked on her nose so that her round face looked endearingly youthful. She put the knitting down as Gemma went in and glanced across at her husband. 'We rather expected you, Gemma. Ignaas told us that Ross had telephoned Rienieta and wanted to speak to you—he wants her to go to Utrecht, I expect. He was talking of it . . .'

Gemma explained and added that Ross had said that he might arrive later in the evening, and his father put down his book to say: 'Much better if he comes tonight, then you can make an early start in the morning. I said that I would bring you back, he'll be far too busy—some lecture or teaching round, I forget which. Did he say if he's spoken to Doctor Kasten?'

'I think he must have done, because he said Doctor Kasten had telephoned him.'

The old doctor nodded. 'Good. I'll wait up; Ross is almost certain to come tonight and we shan't have time to talk in the morning.'

He smiled at her and then glanced at his wife and smiled at her too—quite a different smile, Gemma noticed; tender and loving and very faintly amused. She supposed that the professor would smile in just the same way at his wife when he got himself one.

She explained about Rienieta wanting to see her mother and the doctor got up to open the door for them. Nice, thought Gemma, following Mevrouw Dieperink van Berhuys up the staircase, to have doors opened for you and things picked up for you when you dropped them and someone to smile at you like that ... it would be lovely to go through life with someone who smoothed the rough edges and cherished you. It was no wonder that the little lady sailing along ahead of her looked so happy and contented; a devoted husband and children who loved her dearly ... Gemma fetched a sigh and her companion, on the point of entering Rienieta's room, turned round to ask: 'You're tired, child. Did you have a pleasant evening? But too short, I think.'

'It was delightful, thank you, *mevrouw*, but Leo took me back to his house and there were a great many people there.'

It sounded rather silly, put like that, but her companion seemed to understand, for she nodded and smiled. 'People can be a great nuisance,' she said kindly, and opened the door.

She didn't stay long, the question of her daughter's wardrobe was quickly settled and after a few reassuring remarks she went downstairs again, leaving Gemma to settle Rienieta for the night and pack the few things she would need. It didn't take long; Gemma had finished and her patient was fast asleep and she herself in bed before she heard the sound of a car coming fast. Ross had arrived, coming into the house so quietly that she didn't hear a sound. Only much later, while she still lay awake thinking about her evening with Leo and her future and then Leo again, she heard his quiet, slow tread going down the gallery to his room. It was as though she had been waiting for that sound before she slept, for a moment later she closed her eyes with a contented little sigh.

She was up early, seeing that Rienieta had her breakfast in bed before she bathed and dressed. She herself was already dressed in the Jaeger skirt and coral cotton sweater she had bought in Salisbury; its accompanying jacket neatly laid out on her bed, ready to put on at the last moment; her hair was twisted into its usual tidy bun and she had taken pains with her face. She had taken a minimum of things for herself; night clothes, flat shoes in case she had the opportunity to go sightseeing, which she very much doubted ... She went down to the kitchen where Ria gave her Rienieta's breakfast tray, and she was on her way up again with it carefully balanced, when the study door opened and the professor came out, dressed in an elegantly sober grey suit which Gemma judged must have cost him a small fortune. He looked, she considered, eyeing him over her tray, absolutely smashing. She wished him a sober good morning and he countered it with a cheerful 'Hullo' and added: 'Come down again when you've seen to Rienieta, will you, Gemma?'

He didn't smile, only stared at her rather hard, so that she clutched the tray to her and hurried on, wondering why he should look so annoyed, only that wasn't the right word; he never looked annoyed— remote was nearer the mark.

She was back within five minutes, tapping on the study door, to have it flung wide, and as he ushered her in with all the vigour of a north wind: 'For heaven's sake, Gemma,' said the professor in an exasperated voice, 'you don't have to knock on doors!' His voice was so sharp that she said forthrightly:

'And you don't have to take me up so snappily!'

'I'm sorry, and you're quite right.' His tone was silky and he didn't mean a word of it. 'Do sit down.'

Gemma perched on the edge of a large leather chair; they were all outsize, made for large men, she found herself wondering how his mother managed.

'I am glad that I was able to speak to you yesterday evening,' he remarked, still very silky. 'I should have remembered that you would probably be out.'

She coloured faintly but met his cool gaze frankly enough. 'You didn't need to remember anything of the sort, Professor; I've been out on just three occasions and never when I considered that Rienieta might need me—however, if you find me unsatisfactory, I'll go at once. There must be some very good nurses in Utrecht,' she added helpfully.

He didn't say anything at all for such a long time that she sat a little straighter in her chair, wondering what was coming next. When he did speak she was so surprised that she could only stare at him. 'Gemma, I told you that you were a gem of a girl and I haven't changed my opinion; you have gone well beyond the bounds of duty in giving up hours of time to Rienieta—oh, I know all about the endless card games and the chess and the hours you have spent with her before she would sleep at night. You are entitled to a great deal more free time than you get and no one is going to dispute that.'

He paused and she seized the opportunity to ask: 'Then why did you look so angry just now?'

His voice was placid again. 'I have a bad temper,' he observed. 'Now and again it gets the better of me, but it's all right now.' He smiled at her while his eyes searched her face. 'About Rienieta, it may help if I tell you what we intend to do ...'

She listened to his quiet voice discussing hospital procedure, tests, arrangements made for their stay, the time of their arrival; it was hard to believe that this was the man who had so recently shown all the signs of a nasty temper. He was brief and concise and presently she got up to go. He got up too. 'Have you had breakfast? Nor have I. If Rienieta is still eating hers, I'll see you in the breakfast room in a few minutes.' He opened the door for her as she went past him, put a hand on her arm. 'You look charming, Gemma—you should wear that next time you go out with Leo. Does he know that you are going to Utrecht?'

'No.'

'Would you like me to let him know? I should think you would have an hour or two to spare this afternoon while they're busy with Rienieta, so he could meet you ...'

Gemma studied his face. The heavy lids prevented her from seeing his eyes, but he was smiling and she suddenly had the strangest feeling that Leo wasn't quite real, that he didn't matter at all, and if he wanted to meet her again he could find out where she was himself—there was no reason why the professor should do it for him, especially when Leo had said that they disliked each other. 'You don't like him, do you?' she asked.

The lids lifted long enough for her to see how very blue his eyes were. 'My dear girl, what has that to do with it?' she asked.

She shook her head, not quite knowing herself. 'Nothing,' she told him. 'Do you ever find your thoughts in such a muddle that you can't make head or tail of them?'

'Frequently. What has that to do with meeting de Vos?'

'I don't know—that's what I meant about being in a muddle.'

There was a gleam in his eyes, quickly quenched. 'You would like me to telephone him?'

Her 'No, thank you,' was uttered so strongly that the gleam came back again. She went back to Rienieta without saying any more.

He didn't have much to say to her at breakfast; the conversation was general and in any case

Gemma ate her meal quickly and excused herself on the grounds of keeping an eye on an excited Rienieta. She went reluctantly, though she was enjoying the family chatter going on around her. The professor got on well with his parents and there was a good deal of laughter—the kind of laughter she could share; it didn't make her feel uneasy like the laughter of Leo's friends.

The professor was driving the Aston Martin. He packed his sister into the back seat and bade Gemma take the seat beside his, explaining that Rienieta would be tired enough by the time they reached Utrecht and if she were on her own, would be more likely to sleep. 'So close your eyes, Rienieta,' he begged her. 'I'll stop for coffee on the way.'

He drove with smooth speed, not saying much. Gemma, peeping at him sideways, saw that his handsome profile looked severe and wondered why. But the idle remarks he addressed to her from time to time were made in his usual good-natured manner, and when they stopped for coffee some miles north of Breda, he carried on a light-hearted conversation with his sister which quite belied the profile. They were in Utrecht soon after that, shepherded straight into the hospital and taken without delay to the private wing on the top floor, where they were met by a Ward Sister, a hovering nurse, a grave young man in a pristine white coat and another young man in a short white jacket.

The professor was greeted with respect and wished the entire party an affable good morning before introducing them briefly: Hoofd Zuster

Blom, Zuster van Leen, Doctor Woolff and Doctor Hemstra. He then assured his sister that he would see her shortly, nodded to Gemma and ambled away with various people flying in front of him to open doors. He rewarded their efforts with polite thanks and Gemma found herself smiling; for an important man, and he seemed to be that in the hospital, he was singularly modest in his manner.

Rienieta had a small comfortable room at the end of a long corridor of similar rooms and Gemma had one next to it. There was to be nothing done until Rienieta had rested and had lunch—the professor had primed Gemma about that. She busied herself getting her patient nicely settled in her bed with the magazines her parents had thoughtfully provided, unpacked their few odds and ends and then went back to sit with Rienieta until Zuster Blom stuck her head round the door with the news, in very tolerable English, that Rienieta's lunch was on the way up and if Gemma cared to do so, she could go to the hospital canteen and have a meal herself.

Leaving Rienieta with a dainty meal on a tray and assuring her that she would be only a very short time, Gemma started off down the corridor, through the swing doors at the end and down the stairs as she had been told. She was shy of going to the canteen, for she had no idea whether she paid for her food there or would it be put on Rienieta's bill, and supposing no one spoke English, how could she find out? The professor might have told her, or had he forgotten that she had to eat like anyone else?

She was halfway down the first flight of stairs when she met him, coming up two at a time, to bar her way. 'Hullo,' he said casually. 'I took a chance on you being scared of the lifts, and I was right.'

'I don't even know where the lifts are,' she told him, faintly peevish with worrying about how to get her lunch. 'I'm on my way to the canteen.'

'That's right—with me.' He had turned and started down the stairs beside her.

She stopped to look at him. 'Oh—but I told Rienieta...'

'Zuster Blom will have told her by now that you're lunching with me—we'll go back together. There's a pleasant little restaurant just round the corner from the hospital.'

He marched her down the remainder of the stairs and out of the hospital entrance and then down a narrow street which opened into a miniature square lined with old houses, most of which were antique shops. The restaurant was small and dim and fairly full, but there was a table in a corner for them and Gemma seated herself with a small sigh of pleasure. The room was panelled in some sort of dark wood and there was a large tiled fireplace and no more than half a dozen tables, each with its stiffly starched tablecloth and well polished silver and glass. It undoubtedly had the edge on the canteen.

'I thought you might be a little shy of being on

your own in the canteen,' explained her companion, and Gemma, murmuring suitable thanks, found herself wishing that he had asked her for her company and not out of kindness. 'And I'm not being kind,' he continued, unerringly reading her thoughts so that she coloured faintly. 'I wanted to have lunch with you.'

'Oh,' said Gemma, and regretted her inability to give a clever answer to such a remark; Mandy or Phil would have known exactly what to say. But the professor didn't look as though he expected her to say more, only inquired if she would like sherry and ordered a Jenever for himself. 'They'll start on Rienieta at half past two. I've a full afternoon until five o'clock, so if you wouldn't mind being around? She's scared, though I can't think why, unless she managed to get hold of some medical book or other and read up all the complications she could have had and didn't. Reassure her if you can. She has complete confidence in you, Gemma—and she likes you.'

'I'll do my best. If she gets the all clear today, will she be able to ... that is, you won't want me any more?'

He looked at her over the menu he was studying. 'You want to know when you can return home? Are you so anxious to go?' His eyes narrowed. 'No, how stupid of me, you want to know how much time you have in which to be with de Vos.'

She pinkened. 'It sounds horrid put like that, but I suppose that's what I was thinking.' She added accusingly: 'How selfish you make me out to be!'

127

She glowered at him and he made matters worse by laughing at her.

'Indeed, I had no intention—don't look like that, Gemma. Have you forgotten that I promised you that I wouldn't stand in your way with de Vos? None of us would.' He assumed a look of concern which she didn't think was genuine. 'Why, only this morning, I offered to telephone him ...'

'Yes—well, never mind that now,' she begged him hastily. 'There's really no need for you to bother yourself about me—I'm quite capable ...'

'No bother,' he assured her airily. 'You have only to call upon me.' He gave her a bland smile. 'And now what would you like to eat? Have you tried our herrings—one for starters, perhaps and then how about Steak Orloff?'

They didn't talk of Leo again. The professor was a surprisingly good talker when he chose to be and Gemma found herself relaxing under his gentle flow of small talk and the delicious food. She ate it with appetite, rounding off the meal with a plate of *poffertjes* and a large bowl of whipped cream and observing when she had finished, 'That was one of the nicest meals I've ever had.' She looked around her. 'This is a delightful place.'

'There are equally delightful restaurants in all our big cities,' he assured her. 'I daresay that sooner or later you will visit them all,' and before she could challenge this remark: 'I'm afraid that we must go back to the hospital, much as I regret it ...'

He was two men, she decided; the placid friendly one who had fetched the sausages for her and hung out the washing to the manner born, and this suave, elegant host who was so clearly perfectly at home in exclusive restaurants. It was as they were walking back down the narrow street once more that she asked: 'What did you mean—that I should visit most of the restaurants?'

'Just exactly what I said, dear girl, and if that is another question burning the end of your tongue, let me assure you in your cryptic English: Wait and see.'

They were going through the hospital doors as he spoke. He stopped just inside them, nodded to a group of white-coated young men and women obviously waiting for him, said: 'I shall see you later, Gemma,' and gave her the gentlest of shoves towards the stairs. She went at once without a word; this would be one of his teaching rounds and she knew better than to delay him.

Rienieta was waiting for her and a little disappointed about not seeing Ross. 'A teaching round,' explained Gemma cheerfully. 'And now are we all ready for the first of the tests?' She chattered on cheerfully, bolstering up Rienieta's spirits with a nice mixture of elder sisterly advice and professional know-how so that, by and large, the afternoon went smoothly enough. By five o'clock everything had been done and dealt with and the patient was back in her room, sharing a tray of tea with Gemma.

'I have been good?' she asked. 'I have done what I was told to do without fuss and not made a nuisance of myself?'

'You've been quite super,' declared Gemma

warmly, 'a splendid patient.'

'Then I shall ask for a new dress—I shall tell Papa that you are pleased with me and he will allow me to go to that dear little boutique and choose what I want. I should also like a handbag. I could go to Wessel's—they have the very best ...'

The tests were over, but the results wouldn't be known until the next morning; Gemma was relieved that her companion's thoughts were so nicely diverted. The pair of them were deep in a discussion as to the merits of calf over suede when the professor walked in.

He received his sister's rapturous greeting with tolerant affection, at once agreed that a new handbag was an absolute necessity, and endeared himself still more to her by offering to take her to Wessel's so that she might choose one. 'Let me see,' he mused, 'I'm free from ten o'clock until about midday—I'll fetch you and bring you back here so that we can learn the results of your tests and so on before Vader gets here.' He sat down and stretched his legs. 'Will that do?'

'Oh, Ross, you are my favourite brother—may I buy exactly what I want?'

'Exactly, *lieveling*. Are you tired?'

Rienieta considered the question. 'Perhaps, a little. Zuster Blom says that I must go to bed early. Gemma must be tired too, for she has been here all the afternoon.'

Gemma disclaimed all idea of tiredness, however. 'I'm bursting with energy,' she protested. 'I've done nothing all day—I could walk for miles.'

'How providential—perhaps you will take pity on me and keep me company for dinner, and if you're so bent on walking, there is plenty to see in Utrecht and it is a pleasant evening.'

Gemma hesitated. She had hoped—still hoped, that Leo would somehow have heard where she was and come to see her, even if only for a little while. There was nothing much for her to do once Rienieta had been settled for the night and there were nurses enough if she should want anything. 'Always provided, of course, that you have no other engagement,' said the professor slowly.

'Well—no. Actually I haven't. It's very kind of you—if Rienieta doesn't mind . . .?'

Rienieta yawned to make her emphatic: 'I do not mind, Gemma,' even more emphatic. 'But you do not go at once? You will stay for a little while?'

'I'll be back about seven o'clock,' said her brother, and got to his feet. 'Goodnight, little sister. I'm going to telephone Mama and then I have some work to do.' He strolled to the door. 'Gemma, walk to the stairs with me, will you?'

In the corridor she asked anxiously: 'Is it about Rienieta? Is something wrong?'

'No, and I don't think anything will be—there is every sign that she is completely free of brucellosis, although we can't be positive until the result of the tests. Gemma, will you promise me something? You have been hoping that de Vos might come, have you not? Should he do so, I want you to feel free to spend your evening with him.'

She said awkwardly, taken by surprise: 'I—I

don't suppose he will—it was only a silly idea of mine. How did you guess?' She looked away from him. 'Anyway, I couldn't do that. I've just said I'd go out with you, Professor.'

'My name is Ross, I told you that a long time ago, and I should consider myself a very mean-spirited fellow if I held you to your word—I'm a poor substitute for Leo.' His voice was very even.

'You're not!' said Gemma hotly. 'You're not a poor substitute for anyone, ever—you're— you're...'

'Spare my blushes, dear girl, and just give me your promise.'

She promised in a troubled little voice.

Leo arrived at five minutes to seven, as she and the professor were crossing the hospital entrance hall. It was the professor who spoke in a quite un-ruffled voice.

'Just in time, de Vos,' he observed. 'I was about to take Gemma out to dinner and show her something of the city, but now that you are here, I can feel free to hand her over to you for an hour or so.'

He smiled down at Gemma, who was racking her brains for something to say; it was absolutely mar-vellous to see Leo, of course, but wasn't the pro-fessor giving her up too willingly? She felt vaguely that she was being treated as a parcel, handed from one to the other ... perhaps he was relieved to be shot of her. All the same she asked: 'Couldn't you come with us?' and didn't see Leo's quick frown.

The smile widened. 'How kind of you to sug-gest it, but I have a lecture to prepare and shall welcome the opportunity to do so in peace and quiet.'

He nodded casually at them both and walked back across the hall and into one of the passages leading from it. Gemma watched him go, a prey to mixed feelings. So he wanted peace and quiet, did he? Probably he was overwhelmingly relieved that she should be taken off his hands at the last minute; had merely offered to take her out of kindness. She choked on humiliation and rage, quite forgetting the promise she had made earlier that evening, and smiled brilliantly at Leo. 'However did you discover that I was here?' she asked.

Leo took her arm. 'I have my spies,' he told her laughingly. 'Let's go somewhere gay and eat, shall we? I'm looking forward to a wonderful evening.'

Gemma agreed quickly, aware that that wasn't quite true; it should have been a wonderful evening, but somehow the professor had spoilt it for her. He was a tiresome man, she told herself, and got into Leo's car, carrying in her head a vivid picture of him sitting alone in some dreary room, surrounded by dry-as-dust books and with no one to talk to. She had to remind herself that it was sheer imagination on her part before she could dispel the picture.

CHAPTER SEVEN

Gemma was taken to an Indonesian restaurant in a semi-basement under one of the lovely old houses in the heart of the city. It was hung with silk paintings and lighted by paper lanterns, and Leo ordered a variety of spicy dishes for her to sample. He was at his most charming, displaying an unexpected interest in Rienieta and an even greater interest in herself. He was cheerful too, but it was as though he wanted her to see that he had a serious side to his character as well as the lighthearted one he usually displayed. He listened to her brief account of her day and protested: 'My poor darling, you do have a dull time of it—absolutely no fun at all!'

She looked uncertain. 'Well, I don't know what you mean by fun—I've enjoyed it, actually; Rienieta is a darling, you know, and the family are marvellous.'

'Even Ross?' Leo was half smiling at her in a tender way which made her forget everything and everyone else. She said: 'Even Ross,' and then remembered how he had been prepared to waste his evening on her. She had been cross about it at the time, but now she felt a pang of pity for him. The picture she had conjured up of him sitting alone with his dreary lecture returned more vividly than before. Try as she might she couldn't quite make herself believe that the professor had no other interest in life but his work.

'What are you thinking about?' asked Leo, and then with narrowed eyes: 'Or who?'

She didn't answer that but said instead: 'I expect to go back to England in a week's time, perhaps less than that.'

He waved the waiter away, and Gemma, who would have liked a dessert after all that spicy food, felt faint annoyance at his action—he could at least have asked her; she couldn't imagine the professor doing that ... She didn't pursue the thought as Leo exclaimed: 'I know what I shall do! I shall give a party—a summer evening party—it is a little early in the year to have one, perhaps, but that doesn't matter. We will have supper in the garden room and hang lights outside and everyone can stroll round in the garden, and later we can dance.'

A farewell treat? Gemma thought it might well be and then felt a surge of excitement as he went on: 'Of course, we must see a lot more of each other —when will you be free again?' He frowned. 'We never seem to have more than an hour or two ... What about this weekend?'

'Well, nurses don't have weekends when they're on cases, not regular ones ...'

He looked amused and she wondered why. 'Oh, never mind—a day perhaps, or even half a day. Surely you're able to manage that?'

She looked doubtful but said that she would try. If Rienieta was pronounced cured, she wouldn't need a nurse any more, only someone to keep a check on her temperature and observe her health for a few more days—anyone in her family could do that, but Gemma thought that the professor might expect her to stay and do it. There was a possibility, a faint one it was true, that Rienieta might become ill again, and he would want to guard against that.

Leo was watching her; he wasn't quite sure of her —not yet, but if he could get her alone for several hours it would be fun to get her to admit that she had fallen in love with him. He was beginning to regret his sudden impulse to attract her. She was a nice enough girl even though she was plain, but like most nice girls he had known, she tended to be quite unexciting; besides, she was a complete stranger to his way of life. It had been amusing at first and his friends had found it good sport ... He caught her eye across the table and smiled delight-fully at her. 'Let's go somewhere and dance,' he suggested, 'just for an hour.'

He took her to the Holiday Inn, but not even the champagne he ordered or the excellence of the dance floor deterred her from asking him to be taken back to the hospital after an hour or so. Leo was too clever to show his irritation. He drove her straight there without demur, wished her exactly the right kind of goodnight, displaying just the right amount of eagerness to see her again while at the same time displaying a flattering reluctance to say goodbye. Gemma floated into the hospital, her eyes shining, her world a-glow, and the professor, watch-ing her from the doorway of the consultants' room, noted her flushed cheeks and sparkling eyes and sighed soundlessly.

She was half way across the hall before she turned her head and saw him and stopped to say: 'My goodness, you are up late! Didn't the lecture go well?'

The professor, who never had trouble with the preparation of his lectures, indicated that it had absorbed his evening. He made no effort to move from his lounging position by the door and after a moment's hesitation, Gemma walked across to him, driven by some impulse to tell him about her evening, and at the same time tell him that she was sorry not to have spent it with him. She stopped herself in time, however, for that would have sounded silly, and said baldly: 'We went to an Indonesian restaurant. I wish you had been with us.'

'My dear Gemma, how kind of you to say that, but I hardly think de Vos would agree with you.'

'No—well, perhaps not.' She felt uncomfortable under his steady gaze. 'We went on to a place called the Holiday Inn.

'You're back early,' he observed mildly.

'It's midnight,' she pointed out, 'and I told Rienieta that I wouldn't be away too long.' She flushed a little. 'I like her.'

'I know that. She's going to miss you—don't be in too much of a hurry to go, Gemma. I know there is no nursing to do, but you are a splendid companion for her and you're giving her back her confidence.'

'I'm glad.'

His voice was smooth. 'You have lost a good deal of free time during the last week or so, haven't you?

We must see that you have a couple of days to yourself during the next week.' He smiled thinly. 'I'm sure Leo has asked you for another date.'

She smiled widely. 'Oh, yes—I told him I might have a half-day, and he's going to give an evening party. Would you mind if I went to it?'

The professor's lips twisted wryly. 'Why should I mind?'

Somewhere close by the church clocks chimed the half hour and immediately after that there was the sound of quiet feet and rustling—the night nurses were going to first dinner. 'I'd better go,' said Gemma, and felt surprisingly reluctant to do so. She said diffidently: 'I'm truly sorry about this evening, though I expect you were quite glad to have the time to spare for your lecture.'

He agreed gravely, not disclosing the fact that he had scribbled the salient points of it in his abominable scrawl in ten minutes flat and spent the remainder of the evening with his mind totally engrossed in a quite different matter.

'Goodnight, then,' said Gemma.

And 'Goodnight,' said the professor, only he didn't stop there, he caught her close and kissed her so soundly that she had no breath left to do more than utter a squeak of surprise. She was already up the first flight of stairs before remarks suitable to such an occasion began to enter her bewildered head, and by then it was too late to utter them.

She awoke feeling apprehensive about meeting the professor after breakfast; it destroyed her appetite, so that the loss of it drew sympathetic glances and remarks from the nurses in the canteen, and even Rienieta, never the most observant of girls, remarked on her distraite air. 'You are worried?' she wanted to know. 'You look as though you are going to be sick.'

Gemma mumbled about the rich Indonesian food she had eaten and took care to have her back to the door when the professor arrived, but she need not have worried; he wished her a good morning in his usual casual fashion, suggested that they might as well go at once to the shops, and swept both girls into the lift and out into the street. Wessel's shop was close by and the three of them walked the short distance in the morning sunshine, and spent all of half an hour in its luxurious interior while Rienieta hesitated between a variety of handbags. Her brother, showing no signs of impatience, sat at his ease, apparently half asleep, while the two girls weighed up the advantages and disadvantages of the selection spread before them, but presently he suggested that as Rienieta couldn't make up her mind between a green suede shoulder bag and a brown calf model, it might be as well if she had both. A simple solution but a rather expensive one, thought Gemma, who would have liked either one for herself. She tore her eyes from a particularly pretty brown patent leather clutch purse, and found the professor's eyes fastened upon her so intently that in a fever of anxiety that he might feel it incumbent upon him to purchase it for her, she hurried across the shop to examine some quite dreary shopping bags with an air of nonchalance which brought a gleam of amusement to his eyes.

They had coffee before returning to the hospital, at a large, crowded café which the professor had obviously chosen in order to please his sister, who would have stayed there all the morning if he hadn't pointed out goodhumouredly that he had work to do. They gained the hospital in excellent humour, with Gemma quite recovered from her awkward feelings at seeing him again, and went at once to discover the results of Rienieta's tests and examination. The consultant physician they were to see was elderly, a shade pompous and tiresomely long-winded. He had a few words with the professor after an exchange of civilities and the latter came back with a cheerful: 'Well, you're cured, Rienieta! Another few days finding your feet and then back to your studies, my girl.' He looked at his watch. 'I must be off.' He kissed her briefly, nodded absently in Gemma's general direction, and disappeared, leaving them to drink more coffee with Zuster Blom until Doctor Dieperink van Berhuys arrived to drive them home.

'Well, that's that,' thought Gemma regretfully as she followed the others to the lift. 'Whatever Ross says, there's no reason for me to stay for more than another few days.' She would go back home and never see Leo again, unless of course he had anything to say to her before she went—there was the party, and he had suggested that they must meet again before that. She brightened at the thought and began to plan what she would wear—something new would have been nice and she had enough

140

money to buy a new outfit. On the other hand if she did that, the washing machine would have to be put off for months. Besides, she hadn't a job to go to and she wasn't going to sponge on Cousin Maud. Perhaps the clothes she had would do.

Leo telephoned that evening. Rienieta had just gone to bed, tired and over-excited, and Gemma had gone to the library to write a letter home, preparing them for her return. She was half way through it when Ignaas came to tell her that he had put the call through to her there.

'Which day is it to be?' asked Leo. 'The party's at the end of the week and of course you're coming to that, darling, but what about tomorrow? or the day after?'

'The day after, I think—I haven't asked yet. Besides, I think Rienieta should be kept quiet for a day, and if I'm with her ... I could be free after lunch.'

'For the rest of the day? Splendid. I'll take you to Amsterdam and show you round. Can you get a key?'

'Get a key? Why?'

He laughed. 'So that you can get in, my darling idiot.'

'But Ignaas never goes to bed before midnight—he told me so. He'll let me in.'

'Midnight? Be your age, Gemma—we'll probably still be in Amsterdam until two or three in the morning.'

'Then I don't think I want to ...'

He was quick to lull her thoughts. 'O.K., sweetheart, we'll leave in good time and you'll be back in your bed at a respectable hour.'

'Thank you, Leo. What time shall I be ready?'

'You said after lunch? Two o'clock? It's only a hundred and forty kilometres to Amsterdam and a good road, we'll be able to get up some speed—'bye for now.'

Gemma slept dreamlessly; life had never been so wonderful and it looked just as wonderful the next morning. She and Rienieta went for a leisurely cycle ride after breakfast, round and about the country roads running between the green fields. It was warm, but there was a breeze too, dishevelling her hair and giving her cheeks a nice colour; she could have gone on for hours, but mindful of Rienieta she suggested that a visit to the stables to see how the puppies were might be fun, and her companion agreed eagerly. They had their coffee, brought by a willing Ignaas, at the stables with the little beasts tumbling all around them, and then lay on a convenient pile of hay in the sun. They were on their way back to the house when they met Ross, strolling across the lawn to meet them. Rienieta greeted him with a shout of pleasure. 'Ross, how lovely! You have never been to see us so many times for years and years—are you taking a holiday from your work? Are you staying?' She went on eagerly: 'We could go out this afternoon—you and me and Gemma?'

He shook his head. '*Lieveling*, I'm on my way to Brussels and I'm only here for lunch. What have you been doing with yourself?'

He addressed his sister, but it was Gemma he looked at.

'We went on our bikes,' Rienieta told him happily, 'and then we played with the puppies, and this afternoon, after I've had a rest, we're going on the lake—Gemma knows how to row . . .'

'And is Gemma to have no time to herself?'

His sister looked taken aback. 'I don't know.' She looked at Gemma. 'Gemma?'

'Oh, I'm quite content,' said Gemma cheerfully, 'and tomorrow I'm going out after lunch.' And even though the professor showed not a vestige of interest, she went on: 'With Leo—he's taking me to Amsterdam to see the sights. He's promised to bring me back here by midnight.'

The professor glanced at her briefly. 'I'm sure you will enjoy that,' he said formally. 'And now shall we go in to lunch?'

Gemma didn't see him alone again. The Jaguar slid away from the house directly lunch was over and he didn't look back, although he must have seen her standing outside the drawing room windows. She wished vaguely that she was going with him before allowing her thoughts to return to Leo once more.

The next day was glorious. She put on the jersey dress and hoped that Leo wouldn't notice that she had worn it before and was flattered when he cried: 'Hullo, my lovely,' and then felt completely deflated by his: 'You've worn that dress before, haven't you? Haven't you anything else?' Perhaps the look on her face warned him, for he added:

'You look lovely in it anyway.'

Her world was back on an even keel once more; she smiled warmly at him, returned his kiss a little shyly and slid into the seat beside his.

Thinking about it later, she couldn't remember what they had talked about, but they had laughed a lot and Leo had set himself to captivate her with his own particular brand of charm and gaiety. They were in Amsterdam before she realised that they were anywhere near it, and she looked about her with interest as he drove through the narrow streets, bustling with life. He had a parking place, he told her smugly—the garage of someone he knew. From there it was only a short walk to the Hotel Doelen, where he had suggested that they might go to the open-air restaurant and have tea. Gemma would have liked time to stroll through the city and look about her. There was so much to see—quaint houses, quiet canals, tree-lined and ageless, with their floating flower-shops, and fairylike bridges, but Leo hurried her along; obviously such things held no novelty for him.

But once they were drinking their tea, she was content enough to sit and watch the world go by and listen to her companion's amusing talk. The nagging thought that while they were sitting there she could have been looking at the Rijksmuseum, Rembrant's house, the little Museum of Our Lord in the Attic, the royal palace and the Begijnhof, let alone take a trip through the canals on one of the sight-seeing boats, clouded her afternoon a little; the sneaking idea that if it had been Ross opposite her instead of Leo, he would have made it his business to ask her what she wanted to do and see and then made sure that she was able to do both was something she firmly refused to think about. She was with Leo and that was all that mattered, and when they had finished their tea and she had hinted that she would like a quick look at the palace and see the Dam Square, she allowed herself to be squashed with an: 'Oh, lord, darling, you can't possibly want to go sightseeing—Tourists ...' He shrugged, implying that they were something quite outside his world.

'I'm not a tourist,' protested Gemma, 'and I may never have another chance to see Amsterdam.'

'Don't you worry your pretty head about that.' He took her arm. 'Now we're going to stroll along to the Swarte Schaep and have a drink. We'll eat there later and then visit around ...'

'Visit around?'

'You'll see.'

Their meal took a long time. By the time they had had a drink, ordered and then sat down to eat it, it had turned nine o'clock. Dusk, fretted Gemma silently, and she had seen nothing of the city, only the inside of a restaurant and a café. She wasn't going to see more than that for the next hour or so, either; they went first to Le Maxim, where they danced and watched the floor show, a colourful, noisy affair, before they took a taxi to the Bird's Club, where Leo was a member. Gemma was quite out of her depth here, admitting apologetically that it wasn't quite her cup of tea and reminding Leo that it really was time they started back if they were to be at Huis Berhuys round about midnight.

Leo laughed a little then, coaxing her to laugh to. 'Come on, darling,' he said persuasively. 'We're only just beginning to enjoy ourselves—who is to know what time you get back, anyway?'

'Well, Ignaas, for one.'

He dissolved into laughter. 'That old man—he's a servant!'

Uneasiness crept into Gemma's head. Leo hadn't talked quite like that before; perhaps he had had too much to drink. She remembered the small glasses of gin he had tossed off ...

'Leo, I'd like to go back now. You promised.'

He agreed with surprising readiness, and during their walk back to the garage where he had left the car, there was nothing in his manner to bear out her suspicions—indeed, he behaved in exactly the way a girl in love would hope for, so that she felt mean for being suspicious, especially when Leo told her how much he was looking forward to their drive back.

They were south of the Moerdijk bridge, with the last village some kilometres behind them and Zevenbergen about the same distance ahead, when the car's engine coughed, spluttered, stopped, spluttered again and died. Leo swore, pressed the self-starter and with the tiny spark of life which returned, eased the car on to the grass divider between the up and down lanes. 'Have to stay like this,' he muttered. 'I can't possibly get enough power to run her on to the shoulder. There's almost no traffic, anyway.'

'No petrol?' asked Gemma. 'Hard luck, but this is a good place to stop—anything going the other way will pass so close we shall be able to stop them easily.'

Leo glanced at her. She was taking the situation calmly enough; he hadn't planned it quite like this, but the best laid plans and so on … With luck there would be almost no traffic for some hours. The heavy stuff from the south had gone for the day and wouldn't start again until the early morning. He slid an arm along the back of the seat and said coaxingly: 'Don't hate me, Gemma. I had every intention of getting petrol on our way this afternoon and I completely forgot it.'

It didn't enter her head not to believe him. She made a comforting comment and looked at the dashboard clock. It wanted only a few minutes to midnight; she would be late back. 'Is there a garage within walking distance? There was a village …' She couldn't remember how long ago they had passed it. 'How far is it to the next town?'

'Oh, miles away,' said Leo airily, 'and that village we passed is kilometres away now. We'll have to sit it out. I don't mind, we haven't had a chance to talk …'

'All this afternoon and all this evening,' she reminded him.

He laughed softly. 'You funny girl, that wasn't talking. There's such a lot to say—your future … You do love me, darling?'

She surprised herself almost as much as she did

147

him by saying that she didn't know; she said it so uncertainly that he could be forgiven for assuming that he was being teased a little, but when he tried to kiss her she said quickly: 'Please, Leo—I was sure that I did—at least I think I was sure, and now suddenly, I don't know.'

'Perhaps this will help.' He had produced a bottle from behind him. 'Champagne, my beauty,' and at her surprised glance, he added convincingly: 'My housekeeper has a birthday tomorrow, I was taking it back...'

Gemma's heart warmed at his thoughtfulness. Perhaps she was being an idiot; after all, she was in love with him, wasn't she? Only he hadn't said that he loved her ... She said in a practical voice: 'Then we certainly mustn't drink it. Look, Leo, I must get back. I'm going to walk to the next village. I might see a petrol station on the way—one of those self-service ones.'

'There aren't,' he said positively. 'What's more, my dear idiot, I'll be surprised if you find anything in Zevenbergen—and how are you going to manage about the language?'

'Oh. Well, couldn't you go?'

'And leave you alone? Certainly not! We'll have to stay here until someone comes along.'

'Would they stop? Will that be long, do you think?' She tried not to sound anxious.

'Some hours, I should think. The commercial stuff comes up from Antwerp round about four o'clock ...'

She spoke sharply. 'Well, we can't sit here all night.'

'I'm afraid we must, my sweet, so let's make the best of it.'

Gemma looked around her, but there was nothing; the motorway was white under the moon, the flat country stretched away on either side of them and there wasn't a light to be seen. Quite suddenly she didn't feel happy; Leo was wonderful and she adored him, didn't she, so why wasn't she beside herself with joy at the idea of spending a few hours alone with him—and he had said that they had to talk about her future, but all she was really thinking about was getting back to Huis Berhuys.

She said in a voice she strove to keep normal, 'Oh, dear, what are we to do?' and saw the headlights of a car coming towards them—on the fast lane, too, so that it would pass within a few feet of them and couldn't fail to see them. 'Look,' she cried, and now she didn't try to hide the relief in her voice. 'Someone's coming!'

To her surprise Leo made no attempt to get out of the car. 'You'll have to be quick,' she urged him, 'it could go past.'

It didn't. The Jaguar swept to a majestic halt beside them and the professor got out unhurriedly. 'Trouble?' he inquired, and didn't even look at Gemma.

'I'm out of petrol,' Leo told him, and she could hear the rage in his voice and wondered at it.

'I thought it might be that,' said Ross, and added something in Dutch. He looked at Gemma then.

'I'll take you back—get into my car.' He opened the door and helped her out and took her arm, led her to the Jaguar and sat her in the front seat before going back to Leo. Whatever it was he said didn't take him long; he got in beside her, reversed the car and started back the way he had come.

'I've broken the law,' he remarked conversationally, 'turning on a motorway.'

He could break all the laws he liked. 'Leo?' she asked him urgently. 'You've left him ....you didn't give him any petrol ...'

'There's an all-night garage a couple of minutes from here; I'll get them to go out to him.'

'But Leo said there weren't any.'

'He had probably forgotten,' he said gently, and all at once she wasn't annoyed with him any more, only anxious to explain.

'I'm glad you came—we were wondering what we should do ...' She glanced at his severe profile. 'We left Amsterdam in plenty of time.' She got no answer, so she tried again: 'Were you on your way home?'

'Yes. I called at Huis Berhuys and Ignaas was getting worried, so I decided to come this way—he was afraid that you might have had an accident.'

'Dear Ignaas,' said Gemma, and then exclaimed: 'Oh, my goodness, I never said goodnight to Leo— I do hope he gets home safely.'

'He will.' Ross's voice was bland. 'Did you have a pleasant time in Amsterdam?'

She welcomed his interest; she must have imagined the anger in his voice. She gave him an account of where they had been and added: 'Of course, I should have liked to have seen the city—the old buildings and the palace and a museum or two, but that would have bored Leo.'

'You enjoyed the night club?'

'Well, no, not exactly. I've never been to one before and it was a bit unexpected.'

Her companion gave a rumble of laughter. 'But you have had a taste of night life, haven't you?'

'Yes—but I don't think I'd mind if I didn't go again.'

They were almost there and he slowed the car. 'You are going to Leo's party?'

'Yes, if—if no one minds. He's coming to fetch me and bring me back in good time. It's rather a lot—twice in one week ...'

'Ah, but time is running out, is it not, Gemma?' he asked softly, and before she could answer stopped the car outside the house.

Ignaas was waiting. He exchanged a rapid conversation with the professor, made a number of tutting noises and shook his head a good deal and went away to fetch the tray of coffee he produced, if needed, at any time of the day or night. Gemma sat opposite the professor, drinking hers and wishing she could think of something to say. Finally she came out with: 'Did you have a successful time in Brussels?'

'Brussels?' He sounded as though he had never heard of the place and she realised that she need not have attempted to make conversation; he was deep in his own thoughts. Gemma drank her coffee quickly after that, thanked him for bringing her back, apologised for the trouble it had given him, and went to bed. She was tired, but not too tired to know that something, she wasn't sure what, had cast a blight over what should have been a wonderful day. Strangely enough, when she pondered it, it had nothing to do with Leo running out of petrol.

Nobody said a word to her the next morning about her late return; questions were asked as to whether she had enjoyed herself, hopes were expressed that the party would be fun, and that was all. She spent the whole day out of doors with Rienieta, contented in the peace and quiet around her. Leo telephoned in the evening, turning last night's small adventure into a joke, not mentioning Ross at all, and yet Gemma sensed irritation behind his laughing voice. Reaction, she told herself, after last night; he must have been worried ... everything would be all right at the party and perhaps they would have time for that talk.

He was in splendid form when he came to fetch her; he praised her pink dress just as though it was a new model he had never seen before, made a lot more jokes about their trip to Amsterdam, and assured her that she was going to have the night of her life.

It certainly seemed like it when they reached his house. It was crammed with girls and men, spilling into the gardens, eating supper at the little tables which had been set up in the large sunroom at the back of the house. Leo stayed with Gemma to begin with and then, when she was asked to dance, disappeared, to reappear presently to take her to a small table well away from the others. 'Supper,' he said smilingly. 'I tried to think of everything you would like to eat. We'll dance again presently, shall we, and then I'll take you round the house.'

She had only drunk one glass of champagne, but she felt a little lightheaded from it. She smiled and said yes and looked at the little dishes of food spread out between them. Everything was going to be all right, the faint unease she had been feeling for days now was fast disappearing. She accepted the glass he offered her, but before she could drink any of its contents, Cor, whom she didn't like very much but who was one of Leo's closest friends, sidled up to the table and bent to mutter in his ear. She saw Leo's faint smile as he listened.

'I'm wanted on the telephone, Gemma. I'll be back—finish that drink and have another, and try some of those bits and pieces...'

She felt very alone sitting there with the tables around her filled with people she didn't know. She ate a prawn vol-au-vent and took a sip of her drink. It tasted of nothing much and she was about to try it for a second time when the professor, materialising from nowhere, took it from her hand. 'I shouldn't,' he said mildly. 'Vodka and champagne don't mix very well. Where's Leo?'

Gemma was so surprised that she couldn't speak for a moment, then she said a little crossly because he threatened to spoil her lovely supper with Leo: 'He had to telephone. He's coming back...'

'Yes? Then take pity on me and stroll in the

garden for a minute or two—he'll find you quickly enough.'

She got to her feet unwillingly. 'I didn't expect to see you here—you didn't say you were coming . . .'

If he found this speech ungracious he gave no sign. 'Er—no. I decided to call in briefly.' He looked around him with a hint of distaste. 'I don't much care for this sort of thing.'

They were in the garden now, a pleasant place and warm in the setting sun. The professor paused at a seat and suggested that they might sit down. 'I've had a busy day,' he confided, and bore out this remark by remaining silent for several moments. Gemma looked around her; probably Leo was looking for her, but she could hardly get up and leave the professor sitting. Besides, his silent company was soothing, although why she should need to be soothed she had no idea. She glanced sideways at him and found his blue eyes on her; even as she looked they assumed a sleepiness which threatened to overcome him at any moment. One couldn't sleep at a party; she began turning over in her mind some suitable topic of conversation.

CHAPTER EIGHT

THE privet hedge behind them was thin and high.
Gemma became aware of voices, sounding very clear
in the quiet evening.

'I shall speak English,'—the voice was a woman's,
'for my French is bad and your Dutch is even worse,
my dear. You are enjoying yourself?'

'But of course—such a delightful party, but tell
me, what is it which necessitates Leo going away
into the house with Cor? And why are they so
amused together?'

Gemma wasn't really listening; she was picking
nervously at the skirt of her dress, trying to think of
something to talk about, since her companion remained so disobligingly silent, but the banality she
was about to utter remained unsaid, for the voice,
pitched a little higher now, went on: 'It is very
amusing—that plain English girl with the funny
name and so dull—she does not excite, you understand? Well, Leo and Cor had a bet that Leo would
get her to fall for him in less than three weeks, and
now today he declared that he had won and they are
settling the bet.'

The speaker's unseen companion gave a little
laugh. 'She is stupid enough to think that he is in
love with her? How can it be possible? She has no

looks and she is also plump—besides, she is good.'

Their laughter was in unison and unkind. 'And now what will he do? He surely has no interest in her?'

'Of course not. I told you, he has found it amusing, that is all. He flies to Curaçao tomorrow—he had everything planned very well ...'

'He is a wicked one.' Again the unkind little laugh. 'And when this girl discovers ... I should like to be there ...' There was a faint rustle of skirts. 'Let us go back and see what is happening.'

Gemma listened to the sound of their retreating footsteps. The colour had drained from her face, leaving it white and pinched; not even the evening dusk could conceal its plainness now. She didn't look at her companion, not even when he stood up.

'I shan't keep you a moment,' he told her in a casual, friendly voice, just as though he hadn't heard every word of the disgraceful conversation. 'Will you stay here? I shall be back very shortly.'

Gemma nodded, still not looking at him. She felt sick; to give way to strong hysterics would have been a great relief, to shout and scream and drum her heels on the velvet turf ... The professor turned on his heel and made his way to the house, shouldering his way through the noisy groups of people in the drawing room, to cross the hall and enter a small room on its other side. Leo was there, so was Cor, so too were a handful of their friends. He paused to look at them, his pleasant mouth thinned and turned down at its corners, and although he had said nothing at all, the group spread out, leaving

156

Leo more or less alone.

The professor spoke genially. 'Ah, there you are, de Vos. I hear that you are planning to go to Curaçao tomorrow. A pity that you may have to postpone the trip—on account of this.' He stretched a powerful arm and caught Leo by the collar of his jacket and shook him like a rat, then stood him carefully on his feet and knocked him down with a well-placed fist on his jaw. He stood over him for a moment, dusting off his hands while his calm gaze roamed round the room until it lighted on Cor. His arm came out once more. 'You too,' he said gently, and knocked him down as well; then without hurry he nodded unsmilingly at the astonished faces around him and took his way to the sideboard, where he poured whisky into a glass and left the room with it in his hand.

Gemma hadn't moved. When he handed her the glass, she took it, thanking him in a high voice and tossing off its contents with a fine disregard for its potency; indeed, she had no idea what she was drinking—tap water, tea, sulphuric acid, they were all one and the same to her in her agitated state of mind.

Her companion's eyebrows rose, but he said nothing, only sat down beside her and flung a careless arm across her shoulders, and presently when she exclaimed: 'I do feel most peculiar!' he suggested that she should rest her head on his shoulder, something she was glad enough to do, and remained patiently waiting until it was sufficiently clear for her to mutter in a muffled voice: 'I have no idea what to do ...'

'Quite simple,' he told her promptly. 'We're going to walk into the house and through the drawing room to the front door, looking the very epitome of gaiety.'

She lifted a still swimming head to look at him. 'I can't,' she declared, her voice peevish with shock and humiliation and sheer misery. 'And I won't.'

With no sign of impatience he reiterated: 'Yes, you will. Where's your pride? Pull yourself together, girl—and where's that phlegm peculiar to the English race? Let them all see that you don't care, that you find it amusing too, in a childish way.' He got up and pulled her to her feet. 'Now stop looking like a whey-faced orphan!'

Gemma's eyes glittered with a fine burst of temper, nicely stoked by far too much whisky—it had made her feel sick again, too, but temper, for the moment at least, was uppermost. 'Don't you call me names!' she said belligerently, and then gulped. 'I still feel very strange ...'

'So much the better.' Ross tidied away an end of hair which had blown loose from her neat head and studied her forlorn face. 'Now come along. You don't need to say a word, just smile—laugh if you can; it will only be for a couple of minutes.'

They were almost at the door when her steps slowed. 'I don't think ...'

'Good—thinking won't help at the moment; it's action we need.'

'But supposing we meet Leo?'

The professor allowed himself a faint smile. 'I

don't think we shall.' He was ushering her into the crowded room and she muttered fiercely:

'I don't want to ...'

He cut her short: 'I know what you're going to say: Set foot in this house again. Well, there's no reason why you should, in fact, I'll promise you that you shan't. Now smile.'

It was a command; Gemma did as she was told, and when he paused to exchange pleasantries with a few of the guests, she laughed too. He said his goodbyes as they went, taking his time, while all the time he had her arm firmly tucked into his.

He had said a couple of minutes; it seemed like hours. The open door with the grand sweep of garden beyond became a symbol of escape, the sight of his car filled Gemma with relief. They were in it, driving through the gates and away down the narrow road, when she said urgently:

'I think I'm going to be sick.'

'Only to be expected,' his voice was brisk, 'after all that whisky you tossed off.' He pulled up and leaned across and opened her door for her. 'Shout if you want any help!'

There was a convenient ditch, its steep grass bank running down to clear water. She sank on to the grass and endured the miseries of the moment.

Ross fastened her seat belt when she got back into the car, offered her a large white handkerchief and remarked matter-of-factly that a cup of coffee would be just the thing. 'There's a café down the road, we'll stop.' He shot her a quick, all-seeing glance. 'Did you get anything to eat?'

She shook her head, remembering the daintily arranged dishes of delicious food which had been on the table where she had sat with Leo. She burst into tears and heard Ross say: 'Nor did I. I daresay we can get a *broodje*.' He drove on, taking no notice of her sniffing and snorting into his handkerchief, feeling vaguely resentful because he didn't seem to care in the least that her heart was broken and she was utterly desperate.

The café was open, almost full and poorly lighted in the deepening dusk, so that Gemma's face was hardly noticeable. She was walked inside, with Ross exchanging cheerful good evenings with the other customers as he led her to an empty table in one corner.

It was surprising what two cups of coffee and a cheese roll did for her outraged feelings, outwardly at least. She replied politely to her companion's desultory conversation, and looked around her, her face calm now, although inside her, her unhappiness was so deep and real that she could feel its weight on her chest. She had finished her second cup when the professor asked: 'Do you want to make plans? Talk? Run away?'

Her chin went up. 'I should like to go back home this very instant,' she told him forcefully, 'but I won't do that—I can't, can I? Just to walk out on Rienieta like that, and your mother and father have been so kind to me—but perhaps they would let me leave in a week's time. She could get someone else by then if she wanted to, I expect.' She paused: 'Would that be long enough?'

He knew exactly what she meant. 'To let Leo and his friends realise that you hadn't been scared away? Oh, yes, and we'll go one better than that. I'll take you out and about so that they will be forced to conclude that his boast was an empty one; that you had been having fun at his expense.' He stared at her so hard that she waited expectantly for him to go on talking, but he only smiled again.

'You're kind,' she told him, her face a little flushed, 'but wouldn't that be a bore for you?'

His mouth twitched. 'Not in the least—I enjoy the occasional evening out.'

'Yes, but not with me . . .'

The twitch became a smile. 'All the more reason to do so at the earliest opportunity, Gemma. To-morrow evening—I'll call for you about seven o'clock—and wear that dress, it's pretty.'

Even in her unhappiness, his remark pleased her. 'Yes, well, thank you—if you're sure.' Her eyes, puffy with her weeping, searched his face. 'Why are you doing this?' she wanted to know.

'We're old friends,' he spoke without hesitation, 'not in terms of time, perhaps, but we've done a good deal together, haven't we? And friends help each other.'

It was a nice, uncomplicated answer, and looked at from all angles, it made sense. She nodded. 'It's only for a week,' she reflected aloud, quite failing to see the gleam in his eyes, 'then I shall go home and forget all about it.' She spoke in a wooden voice: forgetting would be hard, it would be like going back into another world. She would have to get a job quickly; perhaps it would be wiser to work in London after all—the future looked empty and dull and she swallowed the knot of despair which was threatening to choke her. She heard Ross say in a comfortable voice: 'Of course you can go home—remind me to see about a seat on a plane for you, but shall we take things a day at a time?' He lifted a finger to the boy who had served them. 'If you're ready to go?'

Somehow—Gemma wasn't sure how—he had turned the miserable evening into a commonplace incident hardly worthy mentioning. Indeed, he said not another word about it but saw her safely into Huis Berhuys, and then got back into his car and drove away with a friendly wave. She stood in the flower-scented quiet of the dim hall and listened to the whine of the car's engine getting fainter and fainter. She felt very lonely.

She didn't sleep at all; the evening's events paraded themselves remorselessly before her resolutely closed eyes, so that when she appeared at the breakfast table, she looked quite dreadfully pale, and the tears she had shed and hadn't bothered to mop had puffed her eyelids and reddened her nose. All the same, she was as neat and composed as she always was and her good morning to Mevrouw Dieperink van Berhuys was just as cheerful as it normally was. 'Rienieta is awake,' she informed that young lady's mother—'she had a very good night and she looks super this morning—she's famished too—she's just about one hundred per cent again. Shall I go to the kitchen and ask Ria to take up her breakfast?'

The lady of the house gave her a brief, smiling glance which saw everything. 'Please, my dear— how wonderful it is to have the dear child well again.' She busied herself with the coffee pot. 'Was it a good party?'

'Yes, thank you.' Gemma took the cup she was handed and made rather a business of choosing a roll from the basket before her.

The older lady helped herself to cherry jam and went on conversationally: 'I'm told that Leo gives splendid parties, though I don't care much for his friends. Did he bring you home?'

'No. Ross did—he was at the party too.'

'Indeed?' Mevrouw Dieperink van Berhuys' face and voice expressed a convincing surprise, all the more remarkable by reason of the fact that she had had a long telephone conversation with her eldest son not half an hour previously. But Gemma didn't know that; she was busy turning over in her tired mind how best to introduce the subject of her leaving. She had her chance when her companion made some observation about her daughter's splendid progress.

'I wondered,' began Gemma, taking the bull by the horns, 'if she would be needing me much longer —she's really well now ...'

'Thanks to you, Gemma. And much as we shall all be sorry to see you go, we mustn't be selfish. I don't know if you have anything in mind, but my sister— the one who lives in Friesland, you know—is coming down this weekend and she particularly asked if Rienieta might go back with her. She would have her cousins for company and ride and sail to her heart's content. What do you think about that?'

Gemma, in a black mood, had anticipated all kinds of difficulties; now there were none at all. She said now: 'I think it sounds marvellous, but I expect the doctor will decide. It's not for me ...'

'He will be coming this afternoon.' Mevrouw Dieperink van Berhuys was quick to see the surprise on Gemma's face and went on smoothly: 'Yes, I know he isn't due to come for a few days, but he is going away. Could Rienieta be in the house after lunch so that he can take a final look at her?'

'Yes, of course, *mevrouw*. She wants to go on the lake and it's a lovely morning. When she's tired of that we could go for a stroll.'

The morning dragged. Gemma, bearing Rienieta company while they pottered on the lake, wandered in the gardens and went yet again to see how the puppies fared, began to feel that it would never be lunch time even while she was aware that the day was beautiful, as were her surroundings, and that normally her contentment would have been complete, but the thought of Leo nagged like a bad toothache. Perhaps it would be easier to forget him once she was back in England and working hard— she wondered if she would forget everyone else too; she would miss them all, especially would she miss Ross. The thought reminded her that she hadn't said anything about him coming to take her out that evening. She did so after lunch, still too unhappy to do more than wonder at his mother's placid acceptance of her news, and her soothing: 'That will be nice, my dear—you haven't been out nearly enough.'

'I went to a party yesterday,' Gemma pointed out. It seemed like years ago.

'Oh, a party.' The older lady's tone implied that she considered that the party in question hadn't been much of a treat. 'A great many gabbling young women,' she observed in her pretty voice, 'criticising each other's clothes and young men with long hair who talk about themselves.'

Gemma laughed despite herself. 'Oh, dear—it was a bit like that, but I thought it was just me; I don't go to grand parties like that at home.'

'There are parties and parties, Gemma. I have no doubt that you will enjoy a pleasant evening with Ross.'

And as it turned out, she did. He arrived a little early, so that when she got downstairs, wearing the pink dress and with her hair and face carefully dealt with, it was to find him sitting with his mother and father in the drawing room, but he got up to meet her as she went in and took her hands in his and held her arms wide. 'Very nice,' he commented in a voice which could have been an elder brother's, 'and delightfully punctual. Shall we go?'

He bade his parents goodbye, made some light-hearted remark about bringing Gemma back safely, and accompanied her out to the car. He drove off at once and without giving her time to speak, said: 'We're going to den Haag—or rather, Wassenaar—there's a dinner dance at Kasteel oud Wassenaar and I happen to know that quite a few of the people who were at the party last night will be there. It's an hour and a half's drive if we get a clear run past Rotterdam. Have a nap if you would like that.'

Gemma was conscious that her day had taken a turn for the better. 'I'd rather talk, if you don't mind. You live in Vianen, don't you? Would you tell me about it? Is your practice there?'

'I don't live in Vianen itself but in a small village close by—I've consulting rooms in Utrecht and Vianen and I sometimes see patients at my home.'

She plunged rather feverishly into more questions; it was a welcome change from her unhappy thoughts. 'Don't you wish you could live at Huis Berhuys—it's so lovely there.'

He sent the car surging along the broad, straight road. 'Oh, very often, but you see eventually it will be mine and I shall live in it as head of the family, but not, I hope, for a great many years. Until then I'm very content and the hospital is a fine one, did you not think so?' He discussed it at some length, giving her no chance to ask any more questions.

It struck her then that she would never see his home; she would be leaving Holland very soon now although he was taking her out it was to stop her being made to look a fool by Leo's friends, not because he wanted to admit her to his private life. Vague regret stirred within her as she listened politely to his description of the new wing which had just been added to the hospital; he was a good talker and she found herself interested despite her preoccupation with her own worries, and presently

166

she forgot them sufficiently to join in a lively argument about hospital management. It lasted until they reached the outskirts of den Haag, and before she had time to feel nervous, he was slowing the car outside the hotel's imposing entrance.

He had been quite right, and she recognised several of the faces turned towards them as they were led to the table Ross had reserved. And it wasn't in a discreet corner, she noted vexedly, but well within the view of most of the crowded restaurant. She assumed what she hoped was a carefree expression and sat down. Ross must have noticed the interest they had aroused too, for his hand came down gently on hers lying on the table between them, and pressed it very slightly. Gemma took it as a gesture of encouragement, although any of those watching them so discreetly might be forgiven for thinking otherwise. He withdrew the hand almost immediately and she wanted to clutch it back again because somehow it made her feel better, but he was asking her what she would like to drink and then there was the business of choosing from the enormous menu.

Until she looked at it she hadn't realised how hungry she was—she hadn't eaten much all day, but now peckishness was temporarily outweighing unhappiness. She decided on hors d'oeuvres, followed by salmon poached in white wine, which she ate to the accompaniment of her companion's pleasantly amusing conversation; indeed, she found herself joining in quite gaily, and presently forgot the carefully casual glances sent in their direction. She finished her delectable meal with a lemon syllabub, drank down the rest of the wine in her glass and jumped up readily enough when the professor suggested she might like to dance. She danced well, she knew that without being conceited about it; the knowledge, coupled with the excellent Sauternes with which Ross had filled her glass, added a sparkle which gave the lie to any speculation and gossip among Leo's friends. Here, apparently, was no heartbroken girl; anyone less heartbroken would be hard to find. Leo had been taken for a ride, they told each other, and Ross, seeing everything without appearing to do so, was well satisfied.

The evening flew by, and it was Gemma who pointed out that they should really leave. 'For we shan't be back before one o'clock as it is,' she observed, 'and I daresay you have appointments for the morning.'

Ross had looked faintly amused and agreed so readily that she wondered if he had been bored; he hadn't appeared to be, but then he had such good manners that he would never allow boredom to show. Her conversation, she remembered uneasily, hadn't been in the least amusing, which wouldn't have mattered so much if she had been pretty enough for every man in the room to envy him. This reflection had the effect of rendering her almost silent during their drive back, and any remarks she did achieve were wooden observations about the band and the hotel. Even her thanks, when they arrived at Huis Berhuys, sounded stiff in her own ears, and his conventional reply did nothing to make her feel easier on that score, so that she was surprised when he got out of the car to help her out and then accompanied her indoors. 'There will be coffee in the library,' he told her, and led the way there.

She watched him pouring the coffee from a thermos jug. He looked calm and placid and not in the least tired, and he was undeniably handsome in the soft lamplight. 'Are you spending the night here?' she asked him.

He gave her her cup and sat down opposite her. 'No—I'd like to, but I've a number of patients to see at the hospital in the morning.'

She glanced at the small gilt carriage clock on its wall bracket. 'But it's awfully late.'

'The road will be almost empty at this time of night—I shall be home in an hour or so.' He smiled at her. 'I have tickets for the ballet at den Haag tomorrow evening—will you come?' And when she hesitated: 'It might be a good idea—this evening was a great success. I can imagine the telephone conversations in the morning.' He added deliberately: 'Leo will be told every smallest detail.'

Gemma swallowed. 'I—I thought he had gone to Curaçao.'

'He has been delayed,' said the professor gently. 'A question of his front teeth ...'

She gave him a puzzled look. 'Front teeth?'

'He lost them yesterday—I knocked them out.'

'You did? Oh, how very kind of you,' declared Gemma with such enthusiasm that her companion's eyes glinted with amusement. 'It's just the sort of thing my brothers would have done.'

'Think nothing of it,' Ross begged. 'It gave me

great satisfaction. I hope you will forgive me when I say that it is something I have wished to do for some time.'

'Oh, well, yes—I gave you a good excuse, didn't I?' She could hear her voice, brittle with false cheerfulness and ready to crack at any moment. She put her cup down and sat looking at it until he said: 'Well, I suppose I must be going. Will you lock the door after me?'

Gemma turned the ponderous key in its lock and shot the bolts and listened to the squeal of the tyres as he turned the car at the gates. Without him, her thoughts became gloomy once more, but she was too tired to pursue them. She went up to bed, her head a fine muddle of smart restaurants, missing front teeth and what she should wear to the ballet.

She had expected not to sleep, but awoke to find the sun streaming in through her bedroom window and Ria standing by the bed with her morning tea. She was one day nearer home, and hard on that waking thought came the one that she would like to stay for ever at Huis Berhuys, wrapped in its peace and security—and that was nonsense, she told herself roundly; what about George and the others and her career? She drank her tea, then jumped out of bed and went along to see how Rienieta was feeling. She was awake and excited at the prospect of a visit to Friesland, so much so that beyond a casual inquiry as to Gemma's evening out, she showed no interest in the subject.

The two of them spent the day out of doors and friends came in the afternoon to join them, and it wasn't until she went to her room to change for the evening that Gemma realized that she hadn't thought about Leo all day—she hadn't had the chance, but somewhere deep inside her she was unhappy, and that unhappiness was made worse when she remembered that she would be leaving Holland in a very few days now. It was no good brooding, she told herself, and self-pity never helped anyone. She would have to grin and bear it until time rubbed it out.

She wore a cream wild silk dress; it wasn't new, but it suited her and its very simplicity rendered it more or less dateless; she hadn't worn it when she had gone out with Leo because it was quite obviously last year's dress and he was observant of such things, but now no one was likely to notice her appearance. She was wrong, for Ross noticed; he came to meet her as she went downstairs and said at once: 'That's nice—and eye-catching.'

Gemma paused to look at him. 'Eye-catching? Oh, I thought ... it's not in the least fashionable, you know. It's last year's—I thought no one would notice ...' Her voice tailed away under his amused look. 'That sounds awfully rude, as though it doesn't matter what I wear when I'm with you. I didn't mean that.'

'I know what you meant, Gemma. All the same, it's attractive, and we want people to notice you, don't we? We have to keep up the good work, don't we?'

'Yes—yes, of course.' She came down off the stairs and walked to the door with him. 'I suppose you haven't heard ...?' Her voice died away and she wouldn't look at him.

'If Leo has been told about our dinner together? No, but then I've been at the hospital all day. But I imagine it highly probable that he has.'

The Koninklijke Schouwburg was packed and they took their seats with only a few moments to spare, which meant that they came under the eyes of those already seated around them. Gemma, conscious of the glances cast in their direction, nonetheless assumed an unconcerned leisurely progress which earned her a whispered word of praise from her companion. 'Good girl—that was very well done,' he said low-voiced in her ear as she sat down, 'and don't look round, but that girl with the teeth who looks like a tent pole is sitting two rows behind us—you remember her?'

Gemma remembered—Lise someone or other, who had sneered at the pink dress. A little thrill of childish pleasure because Ross had called her a tent pole ran through her and she smiled up at him and was disconcerted to meet the unsmiling penetrating look in his eyes; but only for a second, the next moment he was smiling again.

She watched the performance with every sign of interest, not really seeing it at all, her thoughts busy. Surely Leo would have been told by now, and what had he thought? Would he be furious at her apparent turning of the tables on him, or might the whole thing have sparked off a real interest in her in place of the feeling he had pretended so well? Her hands clenched in her lap, as she remembered how well he had done that, and were instantly covered by Ross's large firm hand, and she threw him a grateful glance before concentrating on the stage, this time in earnest.

It wasn't until he was preparing to go after they had returned to Huis Berhuys that he mentioned casually that he had arranged her flight for her. 'I'll let you have the ticket tomorrow,' and when she looked at him questioningly: 'Mama is taking Rienieta shopping tomorrow afternoon; I'll come over for you about two o'clock.' He barely gave her time to agree and thank him for her evening before his own quiet goodnight. She bolted the door after him as she had done on the previous night and felt a faint stir of excitement at seeing him again. He hadn't said where they were going—perhaps to some other public place where Leo's friends would see them; by now surely they would have all realised that Leo's bet had misfired, but perhaps he wanted to make quite certain. Certainly his plan had helped. She no longer felt so humiliated, and Leo would never know now whether she had fallen for him or had been playing his own game. She sighed. Falling in love hadn't been at all what she had expected. She sighed again and went to sleep.

It was raining by lunch time on the following day; Rienieta and her mother went off, driven by her father in the big BMW, and Gemma went to get her raincoat and a scarf for her hair. Not knowing where she was going, she had put on the Jaeger skirt and the coral jumper and a pair of light shoes, and now she looked at herself in the glass and hoped that she would do.

She was too early, but she might as well go downstairs and wait for Ross. He was already there, sitting in the hall, reading a paper. He got up as she went towards him, cast the paper down untidily on to a chair and opened the door on to the driving rain outside. His greeting had been friendly and he made some casual remark about the weather as they got into the car. It wasn't until Gemma asked him where they were going and expressed the hope that she was suitably dressed that he said: 'I thought we would go to my house and then take a look at Vianen.' He glanced sideways at her. 'You look very nice—you always do.'

She felt grateful for his kindness; somehow he always conveyed the impression that she was the kind of girl any man would enjoy taking out, and what was more, she was beginning to believe him. She settled back beside him, already happier. 'I looked up Vianen this morning,' she told him. 'Rienieta was telling me about it, you see, and I wanted to know about the gateways and the Counts of Brederode and the medieval town hall ... are there a lot of tourists there in the summer?'

'Very few, thank heavens. We'll take the motorway, I think, and come back through the country.'

'I forgot to ask your mother at what time she would like me to be back.'

'I said that we'd be back in time for dinner— there's no hurry, is there, and Rienieta's shopping expeditions are time-consuming events, no one will be home before seven o'clock. How well she looks now—you have done her a lot of good, Gemma.'

'Thank you, but I haven't done much, you know. She's a dear, and I'm glad she's quite well again.'

'So am I. She's my father's darling, being the youngest—she's everyone's darling, I think—rather like George ...'

There was so much to talk about; the journey seemed to Gemma to be too short, and she was surprised when Ross said: 'We turn off here. Vianen is another kilometre or so ahead of us; the village is at the end of this lane.'

She hadn't known what to expect, certainly not the delightful house fronting the village square, its ponderous door reached by a double flight of steps, its enormous windows gleaming in the sudden burst of sunshine after the rain. It was flanked by an archway leading to a narrow cobbled lane on one side of it, and the other was hedged off by a high brick wall with a nail-studded door in its centre.

Ross stopped the car at the bottom of the steps, said: 'Here we are,' and opened her door.

'Well,' said Gemma, a little breathlessly, 'I had no idea—I mean, I thought you would have a flat or a little house. This is—is ...' Words failed her and her companion smiled.

'It was my grandfather's house, and his father's before him. Over the years it has been the custom for the eldest son to take possession when he's of age. Come in.'

The door opened under his hand and they went into the long narrow high-ceilinged hall, with its traditional black and white tiled floor, its panelled walls and a number of arched doorways on either side. Before he had closed the door a large, stout woman came sailing down the hall with cluckings of delight and cries of welcome. Reaching them, she clasped her hands across her vast waist, eyed Gemma with small, bright blue eyes, and allowed her strong features to break into a smile.

'This is my housekeeper, Ortje,' said Ross. 'She's from Friesland and married to my gardener. Her niece is the housemaid—all very cosy and convenient for all of us.' He said something to Ortje, who chuckled richly, and when Gemma put out a hand, wrung it briskly and broke into a spate of words.

'Oh, dear,' exclaimed Gemma, 'what a handicap it is not understanding a word! Please will you tell her I'm very glad to meet her?'

The professor said something else and his housekeeper shook with laughter as she led the way to one of the closed doors and threw it open. The room they entered was charming; a combination of muted colours which blended very nicely with the thick patterned carpet underfoot. The walls were patterned too with some sort of silk hanging and hung with paintings under an ornate plaster ceiling. Gemma took the chair she was offered and looked around her. 'It's quite beautiful,' she exclaimed. 'Is your consulting room here too?'

'On the other side of the hall; it can be reached from the door at the side without coming into the house.'

'Was your grandfather a doctor too?'

'Oh, yes, and his father and grandfather before him. We will take a look round presently if you would like that and I'll take you to Vianen before tea—it's not large.'

The rest of the house was beautiful too, its rooms high-ceilinged and furnished with a restrained elegance and comfort which Gemma loved, and presently they wandered out to the car again and drove to Vianen, where Gemma was taken to see the Lekpoort and the Hofpoort and then to view the magnificent town hall while the professor gave her a brisk précis of its history. She asked him anxiously once or twice if he didn't find it tiresome to take her sightseeing, but he seemed to be enjoying it as much as she was, and later, when she had seen everything, he took her back to his house and they had their tea by the open sitting room window, taking advantage of the now brilliant sunshine. And when it was time to go, Gemma got up with a reluctance which caused the professor to hide a small satisfied smile. She wasn't sure now if it wouldn't have been better if she hadn't visited his house, for then she wouldn't have minded leaving it. And she did mind; she craned her neck for a last glimpse of it as they drove away and Ross said: 'You like it, don't you?'

'Yes. I like Huis Berhuys, but now I've seen your house, and I like it even better.'

Her companion smiled and said nothing, and Gemma, her head full of the afternoon's pleasure, was content to sit quietly until he said: 'I'm going off the motorway here and on to the Dordrecht road, we'll skirt the town and take the road to Willem-

177

stad.' He had left the motorway as he spoke. 'There's a map in the side pocket if you want to see where you are.'

She studied it carefully, asking a lot of questions and mispronouncing the names of the towns quite dreadfully. There was plenty to talk about, and they were back, she discovered, long before she wanted to be.

Most of the family were in the house when they went in. Dinner was a gay meal with a great deal of laughter and talk. Gemma looked round the table and knew that whatever else she forgot, she would never forget any of them. She caught Ross looking at her and smiled. She wouldn't forget him either. He had understood how she had felt about Leo; without his help she would never have got through the last few days. For the first time since the party, she slept deep and long.

There were two days left, she told herself when she woke up the next morning, and it didn't seem possible, and today Ross wasn't coming. He had said that he had to go to Amsterdam and didn't expect to be back until late in the evening, and after to-day there would be only one day left. She had been booked on a late morning flight from Schiphol and she tried not to think about it, and was succeeding very well until Mevrouw Dieperink van Berhuys told her that there was to be a family lunch party the next day and of course she would join the family. 'Such a pity Ross can't come,' said his mother, and shot a glance at Gemma's face, which, did she but know it, registered disappointment.

There were a great many guests—aunts and uncles and cousins, the latter all looking very alike, so that Gemma kept thinking that Ross had come after all. The girl cousins were pretty and there was a sprinkling of children and one very old lady with white hair and black eyes. She had a deep booming voice and held a silver-handled ebony stick which, as far as Gemma could see, she used, not to walk with, but to prod various members of her family when she wished to attract their attention. Gemma, feeling shy, was handed briskly round the family until at last she found herself standing in front of the old lady.

'Our great-aunt,' said the cousin, so very like Ross, who was escorting her. 'Barones Berhuys van Petterinck.'

His venerable relation adjusted her spectacles and took a good look at Gemma. 'Nice figure,' she pronounced in penetrating English, 'a *jolie laide*, I see —she'll pay for dressing. Come here, child, where I can see you properly.'

Gemma advanced a few steps. Her 'How do you do, Barones,' was politely uttered despite the old lady's remarks, and she was rewarded by 'Nice manners, too.' Her interrogator patted the chair beside her and waved the nephew away. 'Sit down and tell me about yourself,' she commanded, and Gemma patiently answered the sharp questions put to her until lunch was announced and she was able to slip away to her own place at the table between two cheerful young men whose conversation kept her chuckling throughout the meal.

It was a glorious afternoon; lunch eaten, the whole party scattered into small groups, the elderlies to the drawing room, where they unashamedly took refreshing naps, the younger ones out into the garden and the children to the stables to see the puppies. And because, despite everyone's niceness to her, Gemma still felt shy, she took charge of the children, still small enough to control despite her lack of Dutch. She led the party down to the charming little lake when the puppies palled, and it was here that Ross joined them. 'Got landed with the brats?' he asked cheerfully, and was drowned by the vociferous welcome from the smaller members of the party.

When it was a little more peaceful, Gemma said: 'Your mother said you wouldn't be coming.'

'To the lunch party, no. Do you find my family overpowering?'

'No, not at all. They're all charming.'

'And does that include Great-Aunt Rienieta?'

'The very old lady with the stick? She's gorgeous.'

'Was she outrageous? She's noted for her outspokenness.'

'She called me a *jolie laide*, which is so much nicer than being told that one is plain.'

Ross put his head on one side and took a long look at her. 'There is a difference, you know.' His voice was very deliberate, his eyes on her face. 'No looks, wasn't it—too plump and far too good.'

She went a very bright pink. 'There's no need ...' she began.

'Oh yes, there is, even if it's only to make you see

that you mustn't always believe what you hear. What you are, in actual fact, is *jolie laide*, just as Great-Aunt said, and although this may surprise you, men like plump girls——they like good girls too, Gemma, and don't you forget that.'

He turned away to toss a very small girl high in the air and sit her on his shoulder. 'We are all bidden to drink tea in the drawing room.' He added something in his own language to the moppet on his shoulder, who giggled and shrieked as they went up to the house. The children liked him; he should have married and had children of his own, thought Gemma, trying to keep up to his long stride. Before she could curb her tongue she voiced the thought out loud, then went scarlet and said: 'Oh, I do beg your pardon!'

He had stopped to look at her. 'That's exactly what Great-Aunt has told me a hundred times, and when I told her the other day that I intended to take her advice, she was for once speechless.'

All Gemma could think of to say to that was 'Oh!'

She didn't see him to speak to alone after that. He went away again after tea and they said their good-byes in the middle of a chattering group of cousins. 'I'll drive you to Schiphol,' he told her carelessly. 'The news will get around and there's always someone coming or going there—a last gesture, don't you think?'

'There's no need . . .' she began.

'I have to go to Amsterdam,' he told her coolly.

He had been right again. There was someone there

—Cor, standing with the beanpole, probably waiting for someone. Cor pretended not to see them, but the beanpole nodded coldly and Gemma managed to smile, terrified to look round her in case Leo was there too.

'He's not,' said Ross softly. 'I happen to know that he's in a clinic having some new front teeth put in.' 'Oh,' said Gemma, and then caught her breath as he went on: 'He'll have to be quick about it, he's getting married in Curaçao next week.'

She let out the breath she had been holding and said very crossly: 'Why did you have to tell me that now—and here, too?'

'It seemed a good place.' His voice was mild. 'If we'd been on our own you would probably have burst into tears and flung yourself on my shoulder. You can't very well do that here.'

She had to admit that there was sense in this remark, although she took exception to his dislike of having her head on his shoulder; he need not have said that. She said, still crossly: 'You need have no fear of that; I'm not in the habit of flinging myself at you or ...' She bit her lip, remembering Leo; she hadn't flung herself at him, but she must have done something very like it, because he had felt so sure of her, hadn't he? She swallowed and looked at Ross, who was looking at her with no expression at all. She heard a voice calling her flight and was thankful for it, for she had no idea what to talk about any more. Now she was able to exclaim in a bright voice: 'Oh, I have to go, don't I?' She tried to sound pleased and eager.

She put out a hand and he took it. He took the other one too and pulled her to him and kissed her hard and long. Cor and the girl must be watching, Gemma thought confusedly, and kissed him back.

She joined the queue without looking back at him, and her muttered goodbye was so low that he could scarcely have heard it.

CHAPTER NINE

THE journey went smoothly, which gave Gemma
no reason for the feeling of gloom which slowly en-
veloped her, and it wasn't Leo who filled her
thoughts; it was the memory of Ross's hand crushing
hers in a gentle grip—and his kiss. She had been an
embarrassment and a nuisance to him, and her heart
warmed at the remembrance of his help when she
had needed it most, and the time and trouble he had
spent on taking her out during those last few days,
especially after what he had told her. She hadn't
thought about it much, but if he was about to be
married, he must be relieved to see the back of her.
She felt so forlorn at the idea that she picked up the
magazine on her lap and made herself read it until
the plane touched down at Heathrow. She went
through the Customs and boarded the bus to London without really noticing what she was doing, for
nothing seemed quite real any more; it was like having a bad dream, only she didn't seem able to wake
up from it.

It was when she was standing in the queue waiting for a bus to Waterloo station that the explana-
tion of her gloom struck her with all the force of a
thunderbolt. It was Ross, not Leo, whom she
couldn't bear to leave, and it was he, and not Leo,

whom she loved—had loved all the time; she knew that now with all the clarity of hindsight.

She stood there, unable to think of anything else, while the more unscrupulous of those behind her edged past to take her place in the swelling queue. She didn't notice—indeed two buses came and went before she roused herself to board the third. She had to queue again at the station for a train which wouldn't leave for the best part of an hour, but she didn't notice that either. Anyway, what did it matter if she missed a train—nothing mattered now; she was never going to see Ross again, and she didn't know how she was going to bear it.

She arrived home at last, her head an aching jumble of regrets and far-fetched ideas about meeting Ross again, although none of them really held water, and what would be the use if he was about to get married?

She went through the open gate and up the path and in through the door standing ajar. There were voices coming from the sitting room; she opened the door and went in.

Everyone was there—the entire family—and with them, standing with his back to the empty fireplace and looking very much at home, was Ross.

Gemma dropped the bag she was carrying from suddenly nerveless fingers and gulped back the heart which had somehow got into her throat. 'Ross?' she said in a funny, dry little voice.

There was movement around her. She was aware of the family trooping out, grinning delightedly but saying nothing. When they had all gone: 'You silly darling girl,' said Ross, 'I was beginning to think that you would never know, and then at the very last moment when I kissed you goodbye ... but you didn't quite know then, did you?'

'No,' whispered Gemma, 'it wasn't until I was in the bus queue. How did you get here?'

'I chartered a plane.'

Her eyes flew wide open. 'Ross—a whole plane!' She looked down at her feet and mumbled: 'I didn't know, it's so silly, but I didn't ...'

'Know that you loved me and that I loved you?' he finished for her. 'I know you didn't, dear love, that's why it seemed a good idea to get here first, just in case you didn't discover it on your way here.' He added: 'My dear muddle-headed darling.' His arms, wrapped around her, felt hard and strong but tender too.

She muttered into his jacket: 'But you heard what they said—I'm plain and—and I don't excite ...'

She felt him shake with laughter, but she wasn't allowed to say any more, for he kissed her breathless and then put a hand under her chin to look into her eyes. 'You are my own beautiful girl,' he told her with satisfying conviction, 'and you excite me very much.'

'Oh, Ross,' she said again, then remembered something and pushed him away a little so that she could see his face. 'You said you'd taken your great-aunt's advice and that you were going to marry.'

'You, my dearest, who else? It's been you, ever since I first saw you, all tangled up in the washing.

And why do you suppose Mama gave a lunch party for the entire family? So that everyone could meet you, of course.'

'There were so many of them, too.'

'You have quite a family yourself, my darling— we'll marry and have them all to see us wed.' He kissed her again and paused, his eyes narrowed in thought. 'Let me see, I could manage next week—a special licence could be arranged. Which day would you prefer, my darling?'

'Next week?' Gemma's voice rose to a squeak. 'But how could I possibly—besides, a special licence ... and where?'

'Here, of course—with you in white silk and roses and the church crammed with our families—is there any reason why we shouldn't?'

'None at all,' declared Gemma happily, dismissing at least a dozen good reasons why it couldn't be managed—but if Ross said so ...

The door opened and George's head appeared. 'Cousin Maud said we weren't to interrupt, but it's only me,' he excused himself with a beguiling smile. 'I just wondered if you're going to be married.'

'That is the idea,' agreed the professor gravely.

George eyed him thoughtfully. 'Has Gemma said she will?'

His future brother-in-law assured him that she had. 'Oh, good,' said George. 'I can come and stay with you in Holland, then?'

'Certainly. We shall be delighted to have you.'

George nodded his untidy head; of course they would be delighted. 'I suppose you'll have some babies?' and when Ross said 'Oh, yes,' in a bland voice and grinned at him, he offered: 'I'll play with them if you like—one at a time.'

'A generous offer, George. I believe that Gemma has a present for you in her case—take it with you and have a look.'

When the door had been firmly shut once more, Ross tightened his hold and pulled Gemma a little closer. 'These interruptions!' he murmured. 'How far had I got?'

'Let's play safe,' suggested Gemma, 'and start again from the beginning.'

Did you miss any of these exciting Harlequin Omnibus 3-in-1 volumes?

Each volume contains 3 great novels by one author for only $1.95.
See order coupon.

Violet Winspear

Violet Winspear #3
The Cazalet Bride (#1434)
Beloved Castaway (#1472)
The Castle of the Seven Lilacs (#1514)

Anne Mather

Anne Mather
Charlotte's Hurricane (#1487)
Lord of Zaracus (#1574)
The Reluctant Governess (#1600)

Anne Hampson

Anne Hampson #1
Unwary Heart (#1388)
Precious Waif (#1420)
The Autocrat of Melhurst (#1442)

Betty Neels

Betty Neels
Tempestuous April (#1441)
Damsel in Green (#1465)
Tulips for Augusta (#1529)

Essie Summers

Essie Summers #3
Summer in December (#1416)
The Bay of the Nightingales (#1445)
Return to Dragonshill (#1502)

Margaret Way

Margaret Way
King Country (#1470)
Blaze of Silk (#1500)
The Man from Bahl Bahla (#1530)

Available only by mail!

40 magnificent Omnibus volumes to choose from:

Essie Summers #1
Bride in Flight (#933)
Postscript to Yesterday (#1119)
Meet on My Ground (#1326)

Jean S. MacLeod
The Wolf of Heimra (#990)
Summer Island (#1314)
Slave of the Wind (#1339)

Eleanor Farnes
The Red Cliffs (#1335)
The Flight of the Swan (#1280)
Sister of the Housemaster (#975)

Susan Barrie #1
Marry a Stranger (#1034)
Rose in the Bud (#1168)
The Marriage Wheel (#1311)

Violet Winspear #1
Beloved Tyrant (#1032)
Court of the Veils (#1267)
Palace of the Peacocks (#1318)

Isobel Chace
The Saffron Sky (#1250)
A Handful of Silver (#1306)
The Damask Rose (#1334)

Joyce Dingwell #1
Will You Surrender (#1179)
A Taste for Love (#1229)
The Feel of Silk (#1342)

Sara Seale
Queen of Hearts (#1324)
Penny Plain (#1197)
Green Girl (#1045)

Jane Arbor
A Girl Named Smith (#1000)
Kingfisher Tide (#950)
The Cypress Garden (#1336)

Anne Weale
The Sea Waif (#1123)
The Feast of Sara (#1007)
Doctor in Malaya (#914)

Essie Summers #2
His Serene Miss Smith (#1093)
The Master to Tawhai (#910)
A Place Called Paradise (#1156)

Catherine Airlie
Doctor Overboard (#979)
Nobody's Child (#1258)
A Wind Sighing (#1328)

Violet Winspear #2
Bride's Dilemma (#1008)
Tender Is the Tyrant (#1208)
The Dangerous Delight (#1344)

Kathryn Blair
Doctor Westland (#954)
Battle of Love (#1038)
Flowering Wilderness (#1148)

Rosalind Brett
The Girl at White Drift (#1101)
Winds of Enchantment (#1176)
Brittle Bondage (#1319)

Rose Burghley
Man of Destiny (#960)
The Sweet Surrender (#1023)
The Bay of Moonlight (#1245)

Iris Danbury
Rendezvous in Lisbon (#1178)
Doctor at Villa Ronda (#1257)
Hotel Belvedere (#133)

Amanda Doyle
A Change for Clancy (#1085)
Play the Tune Softly (#1116)
A Mist in Glen Torran (#1308)

Great value in Reading!
Use the handy order form

Elizabeth Hoy
Snare the Wild Heart (#992)
The Faithless One (#1104)
Be More than Dreams (#1286)

Roumelia Lane
House of the Winds (#1262)
A Summer to Love (#1280)
Sea of Zanj (#1338)

Margaret Malcolm
The Master of Normanhurst (#1028)
The Man in Homespun (#1140)
Meadowsweet (#1164)

Joyce Dingwell #2
The Timber Man (#917)
Project Sweetheart (#964)
Greenfingers Farm (#999)

Marjorie Norell
Nurse Madeline of Eden Grove (#962)
Thank You, Nurse Conway (#1097)
The Marriage of Doctor Royle (#1177)

Anne Durham
New Doctor at Northmoor (#1242)
Nurse Sally's Last Chance (#1281)
Mann of the Medical Wing (#1313)

Henrietta Reid
Reluctant Masquerade (#1380)
Hunter's Moon (#1430)
The Black Delaney (#1460)

Lucy Gillen
The Silver Fishes (#1408)
Heir to Glen Ghyll (#1450)
The Girl at Smuggler's Rest (#1533)

Anne Hampson #2
When the Bough Breaks (#1491)
Love Hath an Island (#1522)
Stars of Spring (#1551)

Essie Summers #4
No Legacy for Lindsay (#957)
No Orchids by Request (#982)
Sweet Are the Ways (#1015)

Mary Burchell #3
The Other Linding Girl (#1431)
Girl with a Challenge (#1455)
My Sister Celia (#1474)

Susan Barrie #2
Return to Tremarth (#1359)
Night of the Singing Birds (#1428)
Bride in Waiting (#1526)

Violet Winspear #4
Desert Doctor (#921)
The Viking Stranger (#1080)
The Tower of the Captive (#1111)

Essie Summers #5
Heir to Windrush Hill (#1055)
Rosalind Comes Home (#1283)
Revolt — and Virginia (#1348)

Doris E. Smith
To Sing Me Home (#1427)
Seven of Magpies (#1454)
Dear Deceiver (#1599)

Katrina Britt
Healer of Hearts (#1393)
The Fabulous Island (#1490)
A Spray of Edelweiss (#1626)

Betty Neels #2
Sister Peters in Amsterdam (#1361)
Nurse in Holland (#1385)
Blow Hot — Blow Cold (#1409)

Amanda Doyle #2
The Girl for Gillgong (#1351)
The Year at Yattabilla (#1448)
Kookaburra Dawn (#1562)

Complete and mail this coupon today!